Other titles by

RACHEL LINDSAY
IN HARLEQUIN PRESENTS

Other titles by

RACHEL LINDSAY
IN HARLEQUIN ROMANCES

RACHEL LINDSAY

the marquis takes a wife

Harlequin Books

TORONTO • LONDON • NEW YORK • AMSTERDAM • SYDNEY • WINNIPEG .

Harlequin Presents edition published May 1977
ISBN 0-373-70688-X

Original hardcover edition published in 1976
by Mills & Boon Limited

CHAPTER ONE

'MY dear child,' said Mr Lamb, greeting Beth as though she were a long-lost daughter instead of the girl who had been assistant in his antique shop for six months, nearly two years ago. But in the intervening time they had kept in touch and he knew her father had died and that the Vicarage was being taken over by the new Vicar and his wife, which meant that she, Elizabeth Miller, twenty-five years of age, spinster of the Parish of Westerham, was looking for a job.

'My dear, I'm afraid I cannot re-engage you,' he quavered. 'The lease of this shop is up in a couple of months and I am not renewing it. I am seventy-four, you know, and it is time I retired.'

'I don't think of you as being old,' Beth said with honesty.

'But I am.' He half smiled and then looked serious. 'Were you not left any money at all?'

'A couple of hundred pounds, but that won't last me long. I'm not trained for anything except keeping house.'

'You know a great deal about antiques and, more important still, you have a great love for them. I'm sure you can get a job in another shop.'

'One needs more than enthusiasm these days,' Beth said. 'One needs specialist knowledge and experience. That's why I felt if I could work for you...'

Mr Lamb looked even more distressed. 'I only wish I could help you. Sotheby's do an excellent training course, and if you would take a loan from me...' Mr

5

Lamb stopped as he saw the look on the delicate-featured face in front of him. 'At least let me offer you some coffee while you are here,' he said, and bustled into the back of the shop to make it, leaving Beth to wander around and see what changes had been made in the contents since she had last been here. There were few valuable pieces left and the shop was mostly filled with bric-à-brac. It had been foolish of her to have expected Mr Lamb to re-employ her. If she had paused to think before coming here, she would have realised that at his age he was anxious to lessen his commitments, rather than increase them.

'Coffee is ready,' Mr Lamb called, and she entered his cluttered office and sat on a beautiful Hepplewhite chair while her host handed her a delicate Meissen cup.

'You are welcome to stay here for the night,' he said, offering her some biscuits from a tin.

'I promised Mrs Goddard I would return home.'

'Is she still your housekeeper?'

'She's more of a friend,' Beth smiled. 'We weren't able to pay her wages for years, but she lived in the Vicarage and looked on it as her home. The new Vicar is delighted to keep her—at a proper salary—so I'm glad she will at least be settled.'

'And what will you do?'

'I must give it some more thought,' Beth admitted. 'Perhaps I'll put an advertisement in *The Times*. "Untrained young woman for hire. Docile companion with a fair knowledge of antiques and a great love for them".' She smiled to hide her inner dismay. 'I might get a job, don't you think?'

'Excellent companion with an extensive knowledge of antiques, would be far nore truthful. You must not underrate yourself, child, or other people will do the same.' Watery eyes rested on her with affection, taking in the black dress and coat which did nothing for her pale complexion and straight fair hair. There was a pinched look around the softly curved mouth and the blue shadows beneath the deep grey eyes spoke of worry and sleepless nights. He cleared his throat. 'You will have to be extremely careful how you word your advertisement. I remember I once—My goodness!' he exclaimed. 'What an extraordinary coincidence. I think I may have just the position you are looking for.'

'Oh, Mr Lamb!' Beth clasped her hands. 'Have you really?'

He nodded. 'It's with a dear friend of mine who wrote to me only the other day saying she is looking for another companion. The person she had engaged did not last long, I am afraid. She found the job too lonely, though I am sure it would appeal to *you*.'

'Where is it?'

'In Cornwall. At Powys Castle. It belongs to the Marquis of Powys, though he hasn't lived there for years.'

'Then who——?'

'His grandmother does.' Mr Lamb rummaged in a drawer as he spoke and took out a sheet of thick writing paper covered with spidery writing. 'Here it is. She says she is looking for someone who does not mind a quiet life and has some knowledge of antiques. The Marchioness is writing a book on the furniture at the Castle,' he explained, 'and she wants someone to help her compile it.'

'I've got no experience of that,' Beth said.

'Remember what I said about not undervaluing yourself?' Mr Lamb chided. 'I will write to her at once—or better still, I will telephone.'

Lifting the receiver off the hook, he glanced at the

crested notepaper and dialled the number. Beth returned to the shop, thinking it might embarrass him to talk about her if she were present. She heard his voice—faint and indecipherable—through the half open door and within a moment he called her back.

'The Marchioness would like to see you immediately. How soon can you go to Cornwall?'

Beth hesitated. She would have liked to know more about the job before spending what would be at least ten pounds on the journey. As though aware of the reason for her hesitation, Mr Lamb said: 'Your fare will be paid, of course. How soon can you go?'

'Tomorrow,' Beth said promptly.

Mr Lamb turned back to the telephone and confirmed the arrangements before ending the call. 'The Marchioness will send a car to meet you at Plymouth,' he said as he put down the receiver. 'It's about an hour's drive from there.'

'I hope I'm not wasting her time or her money,' Beth said honestly.

'I didn't tell her anything about you that wasn't true,' Mr Lamb smiled. 'Besides, Henrietta is no fool.'

'It's very kind of you to go to so much trouble for me,' Beth said gratefully.

'It's my pleasure. I'm sure you'll like the job.'

'If I get it.'

'You will. I feel it in my bones.'

Beth's first sight of Powys made her hope that Mr Lamb's statement had been prophetic. The Castle looked beautiful and for ever after she was always able to recall the pleasure she had felt at seeing the grey battlements standing clear and bold against the deep blue sky. Even on a dull day Powys would have been awe-inspiring, but to see it with the sun shining on the rolling green pastures and rich red earth around it gave it a magnificence that took her breath away.

Mr Lamb had given her no hint of what to expect, and because his own shop was old and crumbling she had expected Powys to be the same. But there was no sign of disrepair about the mile-long drive and the well-tended lawns that went up in a rush of green to the flight of wide steps leading to the massive, nail-studded door. There was something foreign about the Castle, as though it would have looked equally at home in a sunnier clime, and she remembered the books she had read as a child about the Portuguese and Spanish smugglers whose ships had foundered of this coast, and who had found temporary safety among their customers, leaving behind more than a few gold ducats as mementoes of their visit—as witnessed still in the sallow-skinned, jet black hair and dark eyes of so many Cornish men and women.

Nervously Beth mounted the steps and tugged at the bell pull. No sound came from it, but almost immediately the door was opened by an elderly butler who must have been expecting her, for when she gave her name he led her across a black and white marble floor into a small ante-room off the main drawing-room. The walls were lined with tapestries and there was a particularly fine carpet on the floor whose muted pastel colours were picked out on the several settees and armchairs which stood around her. Genuine French pieces, she noted, the furniture its original rosy gold gilt and not the bright brassy colour of contemporary pieces. A beautiful rosewood spinet stood in front of one of the windows and, left alone to wait for the Marchioness, she went over and looked at it, marvelling at the intricate inlay on the top and its excellent state of preservation.

'You like the spinet?' The thin but firm voice which

asked the question made Beth turn and she saw a tall, thin old lady coming towards her. She had undoubtedly been a beauty in her youth, for even now age had not dimmed the lustre of the dark eyes nor the fine bone structure of the arched nose, the high forehead and the imperiously pointed chin. The skin was as lined as a dried apple, but the hair that sculpted the head was thick and black, artificially black, Beth suspected, because the density of the colour made the woman look a little like a witch. But a benevolent one, for she was smiling and radiated a warmth that was almost tangible.

'You haven't answered my question.'

The words made Beth realise she had been guilty of staring and she blushed and stammered that she thought the spinet was beautiful.

'It can be played too,' the Marchioness said. 'So many of them you see these days have had their insides taken out and are used as cocktail cabinets or repositories for cutlery!'

'I don't object to that,' Beth replied, 'as long as the piece is appreciated and cared for. Most homes these days can't afford the space to have a spinet that's just played.'

'Just played!' the Marchioness expostulated. 'That remark is typical of the age we live in.' A claw-like hand indicated that Beth should sit down. 'Tell me about yourself. Eugene Lamb gave me no information beyond the fact that he thought you would suit me and that he held you in the highest esteem.'

'What would you like to know about me?'

'Everything. If you are to be my companion, I must know all about you.'

Hesitantly Beth began a résumé of her life. Even given in detail she knew it was unexciting, as was to be expected in the life of an only child born late in marriage to a vicar and his wife. Words alone could give no indication of the warmth and affection of her quiet upbringing; her years at a small but good school and her return from it to take care of her mother after a stroke. Her death, a few years later, had given Beth the opportunity to work for Mr Lamb in London, where she had been able to satisfy her love for antiques by trying to obtain a knowledge equal to it. But her father's heart attack had forced her to return to Westerham again, and she had remained there for the past two years to take care of him until his death.

'That's when I went to see Mr Lamb,' she concluded. 'I hoped I could work for him again, but he's closing his shop.'

'Working for Eugene is no more suitable for you than working for me,' the Marchioness said brusquely. 'We are both far too old for you. You are a young woman, Miss Miller, and you should want more from life than to settle into a backwater like this.'

'How can you call this wonderful place a backwater!' Beth exclaimed. 'It's a treasure house—it would be like living in a museum.'

'That's what I meant,' came the dry answer, 'but obviously you are not like your contemporaries. Still, in one respect you are right. Powys is a museum, though if it had a family and children living in it, it would soon become a home.' The thin voice stopped abruptly and Beth remained silent, instinctively knowing the old lady was lost in sad thoughts. She was mildly annoyed with herself for not having asked Mr Lamb for more information about the Powys family. Why was the Marchioness living here alone? Where was the Marquis, and why hadn't he married, for he must surely be quite old?

'My grandson doesn't care for Powys,' the thin voice continued, unknowingly answering one of Beth's questions. 'He is fond of the place, but it does not mean to him what it means to me. He hasn't seen it for six months and then he only came for a couple of days to see me.' The old lady stood up and walked around the room slowly, partially supporting her weight on a mal-acca cane. 'Do you find his behaviour understandable or do you think—like my grandson—that I am trying to hold on to a dream and wasting my time?'

'I'm afraid I don't understand,' Beth murmured. 'A dream of what?'

'Of making Powys a home again. Of filling the rooms with children and laughter. Yorke says he will never live here. He doesn't even want the title. He calls me an anachronism.'

Beth could find nothing to say to this. Surely it was possible to live in the present without destroying the past, particularly when the past was as beautiful as Powys.

'But I am boring you with stories of my family,' the Marchioness said abruptly. 'If you decide to take the job, you will have your fill of Yorke.'

'It's an unusual name,' Beth murmured.

'My grandson is an unusual man. David Cecil Edward Thomas Yorke, Marquis of Powys. He has never ans-wered to any name other than Yorke since he was a child.' The Marchioness rapped the floor with her cane. 'An obstinate and infuriating child.' She leaned closer. 'Well? Do you think you will be content here? Don't take the job if you are looking for bright lights and lots of companionship. There is only the house and myself.'

'I have no doubt I could be happy here,' Beth replied, 'but will you be happy with *me*?'

'Possibly,' the Marchioness said in grudging tones. 'Let's give it a try and see; a month should tell us, don't you think?'

Within a week Beth felt she had lived at Powys for months, and within a month that she had lived there for years.

The Marchioness had not been joking about her determination to keep the Castle alive as a home, and to this end she insisted that every room was used. This meant sleeping in a different bedroom each week and alternating their meals between the Van Dyck dining room—so called because of the magnificent painting that hung on its walls—and the red rose dining room where practically all that colour predominated, while their evenings were spent between the vast library, the equally vast drawing-room, the music room and the smaller anteroom where Beth had first been interviewed.

It was the changing of bedrooms which she found the most irritating, for no sooner had she grown used to one mattress than she was obliged to adjust to another. Appreciating the reasons for the constant shifting, she made no complaint, but could easily see why the previous companions had not stayed longer than an average of three months. 'But *I'll* stay,' Beth told herself, for she had known from the moment she had seen Powys that it was going to mean something to her. Perhaps it was because she was a romantic at heart that she was so conscious of the romance that emanated from every room and every object. It spoke to her from each piece of furniture and it veritably shouted at her from each portrait of the Powys family that lined the walls of the Long Gallery which took up the entire length of the first floor. Here was housed a priceless collection of paintings, and though Beth admired them all, it was the family portraits that intrigued her the most, beginning with the first Marquis in the time of Elizabeth the First and ending with the father of the present one, resplendent in a Colonel's uniform in the Second World War.

Of the present owner there was no sign, and she wondered if the portraits were painted at a specific time in the life of each heir, for all the men seemed to have been painted in their middle thirties, and all had narrow, aquiline features: a long nose, heavy-lidded dark eyes and black, thrusting hair that sprang away from a high, wide forehead. As always when she spent any time in the Long Gallery, Beth left it with a feeling of dismay that the present holder of the title should have no interest in preserving what had been so lovingly kept for hundreds of years, and she was full of curiosity to know what turn his life had taken to lead him away from here. But since her first meeting with the Marchioness the old lady had not spoken of her grandson, and it was not until Beth's sixth week, when she went into the Marchioness's bedroom with her daily post, that fuller mention was made of him. It was prompted by an airmail letter that bore a South African stamp.

'My grandson is a biologist,' the old lady said dourly, 'and he is doing research at the Mandama Centre in Kruger Park.'

'Isn't that a game reserve?' Beth asked.

'Yes, it's one of the biggest in South Africa. The Mandama Research Centre is situated inside it.'

'What research is your—is the Marquis doing?'

'Something to do with rabies.' The claw-like hands clenched on the coverlet. 'If it weren't for those microbes of his, he'd be living here, where he belongs, instead of in some hut in the wilderness!' She sighed deeply and lay back against the pillows. Only when in

14

bed did she look her seventy-odd years, for at other times she could easily pass for a sprightly sixty-year-old. 'Of course it isn't only because of the microbes,' she added. 'Once Anne turned him down, his obstinacy wouldn't let him come back to Powys. Anne was a fool, of course. One would have thought she knew Yorke well enough not to try and force him into doing what she wanted. You could never get your own way with him if it came to a battle of wills. He has to be cajoled ... led gently ... and instead the stupid girl gave him an ultimatum: if you go to Mandama I'll break our engagement and marry the next person who asks me. Well, what would any normal, red-blooded man have done?' The Marchioness snorted. 'Yorke told her if that was the way she felt she could marry whom she pleased. And she did! Since then he has never set foot in Powys except to see me for a couple of days.'

More than ever Beth failed to understand the mentality of a man who could allow a soured love affair to affect the way he felt about his home. And Powys *was* a home, as the Marchioness so rightly said.

'What will happen to Powys when you ...' Beth stopped, flushing scarlet, but it was too late to withdraw her words, for the Marchioness finished them for her.

'When I'm dead? Yorke will give Powys to the National Trust with enough money to maintain it.'

'But then no one will live in it!'

'What can I do? He is already threatening to sell the pictures that aren't entailed and use the money for his ridiculous research.'

'Is it ridiculous?' Beth asked, anxious to be fair to the man, even though she did not know him.

'Not in itself. But it's ridiculous for *Yorke* to be doing it. His place is here—where he belongs—not thousands

15

of miles away. While I am alive there is a faint chance that I can make him feel guilty enough to come back and give it another try, but if I die before I can do that, then he will never return.'

Beth moved over to the bed, sympathy making her long to comfort her employer, yet she knew better than to put this feeling into words or actions, and instead made an effort to turn the conversation.

'I didn't know your grandson used to manage the estate.'

'This was his base,' the Marchioness said. 'He had his research work, but he was still able to supervise everything that went on here. He had even settled the date of his wedding when he was asked to go to the Mandama Centre for a couple of years. Anne said it was out of the question and Yorke went off alone.'

'Surely the most important thing is that he is happy,' Beth said gently. 'After all, a person is more important than a house.'

'Yorke *was* happy here. If it hadn't been for Anne he would have come back once the two years was up. But she is so closely woven into Powys that he cannot bear to be here.'

'Then you should try to accept that fact,' Beth said firmly.

'I am too old to change my character. I will never accept defeat!' The woman sat up straight. 'Ring for Gladys, my dear. I am going to dress. Then we will start work on the next chapter. I am determined to finish my book before I die.'

Beth smiled and rang the bell for the maid. 'I'll wait for you in the library. I still have a few pages to type.'

But with the manuscript in front of her, Beth sat motionless for several moments, wondering how the

Marquis would feel if he was given the opportunity of reading it. Hard-headed though he seemed, he could not fail to be moved by it. Sighing, she inserted a sheet of paper into the typewriter and began to type.

When Mr Lamb had told her the Marchioness was compiling a history about the furniture in the Castle, she had never envisaged it as being anything more than a detailed description of each piece, and she had been fascinated to find it was also a skilled and perceptive assessment of the life and times of the Powys family. One did not need to be a member of it to find it a wonderful story, for it was also an account of the changing times in Britain.

Beth was on the last page of the present chapter when the Marchioness appeared, and for the next couple of hours she took down the beginning of a new instalment, using a mixture of a few shorthand symbols and her own form of speed-writing. The ringing of the luncheon bell put an end to this, though Beth fully expected her employer to continue her discourse of the eighteenth century Powyses—a rascally lot—if she was to be wholly believed. However, the Marchioness had something quite different to relate, and Beth heard it with astonishment. They were, it seemed, going to go to Africa for a holiday.

'If Mahomet will not come to the mountain,' she said, munching her grapefruit with ferocity, 'then the mountain will go to Mahomet. And you will come with me.'

Beth's heart thumped with excitement. For someone who had only gone to Switzerland on a school holiday, the thought of going thousands of miles to the wild dark continent of Africa was at once both exciting and frightening.

'Gladys is too old to travel and she would get on my

nerves with her chattering,' the Marchioness continued. 'So find out what injections we will need and make arrangements for us to fly out the moment we can.'

Thinking of the injections reminded Beth of her employer's age and she felt duty bound to suggest that the Marchioness's doctor was called in to agree to her taking such a long journey.

'No fool of a doctor is going to stop me,' came the forthright reply.

'But he could stop *me*,' Beth stated. 'I wouldn't want to accept the responsibility of going with you, unless he said you were fit enough to travel.'

'What a fuss you make! These days travelling is nothing.'

'I still think——'

'Very well,' the Marchioness grumbled. 'Ask him to call, then.'

Later that afternoon Doctor Burdon drove over to see his most irascible patient, and then gave Beth a well covered prescription form as she accompanied him to his car.

Dismayed, she looked at it. 'I hadn't realised the Marchioness was as ill as this.'

'She has very high blood pressure,' the doctor said. 'Unfortunately she persists in pretending she hasn't. I suppose it's better than having her go to the other extreme and become a hypochondriac, but I would like you to stop her acting as if she's still in her twenties! She needs plenty of rest, a salt-free diet and no alcohol.'

Beth remembered the glass of wine drunk at each meal and, glancing at the doctor, knew he was aware of this too.

'An occasional glass won't do any harm,' he said, 'but see she doesn't have one with every meal.'

'I'm the Marchioness's companion,' Beth reminded him, 'not her jailor!'

The doctor regarded her quizzically, seeing the delicate features, the long, beige-coloured hair and the small but softly rounded body casually attired in skirt and jumper; all gave an aura of diffidence, yet he saw beneath it to the stubbornness in the chin and the determination that glinted occasionally in the eyes. They were her finest feature, he decided, being large and limpid, and the colour of silver birch. As she waited by the car a beam of sunlight brought pale gold glints into her fair hair and made him wonder if perhaps *this* was her nicest feature. Still, her mouth was charming too: finely chiselled and devoid of lipstick. The doctor mentally gave himself a shake. What it really amounted to was that this gentle-looking young woman had far more depth to her than one first appreciated, not only in appearance but in charater.

'Don't worry too much about the Marchioness,' he said as he opened his car door. 'Don't forget Yorke is a doctor too.'

'I thought he was a biologist.'

'So he is. But he got his medical degree and then went on to specialise. I wish I'd done the same myself. I've yet to hear of a test tube calling you out at three o'clock in the morning!'

With a wave of his hand he drove off and Beth went in to the Marchioness, who was already at her desk making telephone calls regarding their journey.

'I won't tell my grandson I'm flying over to see him,' she announced. 'We'll cable him the morning we leave. That will give him time to book us into a hotel.'

'It's the height of their tourist season,' Beth reminded her.

'Then he'll have to pull a few strings. A title is a great asset in those sort of circumstances.'

'You mean that too,' Beth laughed.

'I mean everything I say.' The dark eyes glinted. 'But occasionally I don't say everything I mean.'

Beth was to remember these words a long time later, when the meaning behind the Marchioness's remark had become all too heartbreakingly clear.

CHAPTER TWO

The flight from Heathrow to Jan Smuts Airport outside Johannesburg was uneventful, though Beth, who had never flown before, found it exhilarating to fly forty thousand feet above the earth, with occasional glimpses of land and sea far below. But for the most part she stared down at what appeared to be a white blanket of cotton wool, and found it hard to believe they were travelling at over six hundred miles an hour.

The Marchioness was unexpectedly docile on the journey, and made no objection when Beth removed the arm rests from between their seats so that she could stretch out more comfortably.

'You were waiting for me to say I didn't want to lie down, weren't you?' she commented as Beth wrapped a pale blue blanket around her.

'I thought you might insist on showing how young you are by sitting up the whole time!' Beth confessed.

'Instead of which I'm showing you how sensible I am by recognising the limitations of age.'

'You're ageless,' Beth teased.

'I'll remember that the next time you order me to bed in the afternoon.'

'I've never succeeded in ordering you to do anything. But thanks for putting the idea in my mind.'

'Take it out again, girl. It won't get you anywhere.' Dark eyes raked the young face. 'You look more in need of a rest than I do. You are as pale as a ghost.'

'I always go pale when I'm excited,' Beth said. 'As a

child I used to look so white that it was all I could do to persuade my mother not to send me to bed!'

'You must have been a nice little girl.'

'Don't you think I still am?' Beth asked humorously.

'You are too old to be called a girl. You are a woman, and it is time you realised it.' The Marchioness closed her eyes and Beth took the seat across the aisle and stared out through the porthole window. The black sky turned it into a mirror and her reflection stared back at her: the face of a ghost etched in glass. It was all very well to be told to stop acting like a girl, but it took more than wishes to turn a girl into a woman. It took a man's love. But men had been few and far between in the village of Westerham, for it was a place from which the young were eager to escape; as she had escaped once death had ended her duty to her parents. Yet it was only when she had come to work for the Marchioness that she had realised the gaps there had been in her growing-up years. Never had she known gay student parties, holding hands in the back row of the cinema or arguing with other young people into the small hours of the night. For her it had been quiet days shopping and keeping house and quiet evenings reading or listening to the radio. Even the television was something she had rarely seen until she came to Powys.

Powys, that wonderful great castle that stood in acres of rich Cornish soil. An empty house whose owner had no time to spare for it. The thought filled her with anger and she wondered what sort of man Yorke Powys could be, that he could turn completely away from his heritage, and what sort of girl it had been who had made him do so. But on the question of her grandson's ex-fiancée the Marchioness was reticent, and her first outburst against her had also been her last. Beth shifted carefully in her seat, anxious not to crease the skirt of her suit. It was a pretty tweed one in a mixture of corn-flower blue and grey, and with it she wore a silk blouse in the same shade of blue. It made her look more fair and gave a warm tinge to her pale skin. It was the nicest suit she had owned and, like the whole pile of clothes reposing in her suitcase, had been an unexpected present from the Marchioness.

'I know your wardrobe isn't equipped for a holiday,' she had said one afternoon when she and Beth were going for a drive, 'so I intend to give myself the pleasure of buying you what you need.'

No protestations from Beth could dissuade her, and she had watched with mounting embarrassment as dress after dress had been ordered.

'I only need a couple of cotton ones and a pair of slacks,' she had said. 'We're going on a safari holiday, not a luxury cruise.'

'I enjoy buying pretty things,' the Marchioness had overruled her. 'And it will give me pleasure to see you wear them. Look on it as an investment for me.'

'It's an investment without much of a return,' Beth had said.

'I hope I *will* have a return,' the Marchioness had re-plied, and though Beth had asked her what she meant, no explanation had been given.

She thought of this now and glanced across at the sleeping woman. By this time the Marquis would have received their telegram, and he was either delighted by his grandmother's unexpected visit or furious at her high-handedness in arriving without sufficient warning. From the little she had learned of him she could not imagine him being pleased, and felt a vague presentiment of fear at what he might do. 'Probably send us back on the next

23

plane,' she thought just before she fell asleep, 'and we'll have had those awful injections for nothing.'

It was mid-morning, eighteen hours after leaving London, when Beth walked beside her employer to the large airport terminal. In a surprisingly short time their luggage was cleared through Customs, their passports stamped by a friendly officer who wished them an enjoyable holiday and they were walking towards a tall, dark-haired man whose own steps covered the distance far more quickly, so that within seconds of being sighted he was bending to put his arms round the Marchioness's angular shoulders and stooping to kiss the wrinkled cheek.

'Grandmother,' he said in a surprisingly soft-spoken voice, 'when will you ever stop surprising me?'

'The day you present me with an heir,' came the prompt answer. 'Then I will obey every one of your orders!'

'That's too high a price to pay,' he smiled, and glanced at Beth. 'You are Miss Miller?'

'Yes.' Beth's hand was shaken by a lean firm one before the man turned back to his grandmother and escorted her across the terminal and out to a waiting limousine. This gave Beth the opportunity to study him and she was surprised to find him older than she had anticipated. But then the Marchioness had a habit of making people seem younger than they were merely by continually insisting that they do as she told them and, because of this, Beth had envisaged the Marquis as a harum-scarum young man messing about with test tubes in the jungle, whereas Yorke Powys exuded tenacity and determination. Here was not a man to be intimidated. His fiancée had failed to do this and so had his grandmother, though she refused to acknowledge the fact.

Only in looks was Yorke Powys the way Beth had believed him to be, for he could well have stepped down from one of the illustrious portraits of his ancestors that hung on the walls of the Long Gallery. Not a recent ancestor though, she decided, studying him carefully, but one of the tall, dark, dominant-nosed men from the seventeeth century, with their velvet doublets and stiff lace ruffles at neck and wrist. Looking at the tanned skin, bronzed even darker by the African sun, and at the thick, straight black hair which, though brushed carefully flat, still gave the impression of springing vitality, it was easy to recognise the Spanish blood in his veins and to imagine that far back in his line there had been a bold buccaneer roaming the high seas and raising the skull-and-crossbones.

'Why are we going to Johannesburg?' The Marchioness's question jerked Beth out of her reverie. 'If you intend to send us back to London——'

'I wouldn't dare!' her grandson replied. 'Anyway, now you are here I expect you want to see something of the country?'

'Something of you,' came the correction. 'Your grandfather and I travelled through Africa before you were born. No, Yorke, *you* are the reason I came here today and I want to discuss——'

'I'm sure Miss Miller dosn't wish to hear our family quarrels,' he intervened.

'I am not quarrelling with you, Yorke.'

'In that case I suggest you look out of the window and admire the scenery.'

'There is nothing to see. It is flat and dull.'

'We will only stay in Johannesburg for a night,' he explained mildly. 'You can go to bed and rest and I'll

25

give Miss Miller a tour of the city. Then in the morning we will fly to the Kruger Park.'

'Fly?' Beth only realised she had spoken as two pairs of dark eyes—both completely like each other—stared at her. She blushed painfully. 'I—I thought it was only a car ride away from here.'

'A *long* car journey, Miss Miller,' Yorke Powys said. 'I thought my grandmother would find it less tiring to fly.'

'An excellent idea,' the Marchioness told him. 'You are very thoughtful about little things!' She gave him a fierce stare. 'You have not inquired about Powys.'

'I'm sure it's still standing.'

'Much you would care if it wasn't!'

'I do care,' he said gently, 'but it's only a house.'

The Marchioness looked as though she were going to choke, but managed to control herself and stared tight-lipped through the window, preferring the flat country-side to an argument.

They were driving through the outskirts of Johannes-burg, with its rows of ramshackle houses which soon gave way to the more affluent suburbs and then the sky-scrapers of the city centre, which zoomed like glass fingers up into the electric blue sky. The sun was an orb of gold directly overhead and the pavements shimmered with heat, but the hotel they entered was cool with air-conditioning, overly ornate with gilded rococo furnish-ings and a superabundance of lampshades. Within mo-ments they were gliding up to the eighteenth floor and a magnificent suite of rooms.

'I wasn't sure whether you slept near my grand-mother,' the Marquis murmured so that only Beth could hear, 'but I thought it advisable for you to be at hand.'

'I'm glad you did. I do try and sleep as near to her as I can at Powys, but it isn't always possible to manage it.'

She saw his quizzical look and said: 'We change our bedrooms each week.'

'Oh lord! I didn't realise my grandmother was still doing that!'

'Your grandmother is determined to keep Powys a home, not a museum.'

'I know,' he said. 'She's wasting her time,' he added abruptly. 'I have no intention of coming back. My life is here, doing research. I have no desire to show gawping visitors round a stately home.'

Unwilling to argue with him, Beth walked through the sitting-room and into her own bedroom. It was ornately furnished in blue and green brocade, with a thick carpet underfoot and twin beds with padded headboards. It could have been a room in any luxury hotel, instead of Johannesburg in the heart of South Africa, thousands of miles from London. This was not the Africa of her imagination but the Africa of a cosmopolitan society.

'Your room tomorrow night won't be like this.' She swung round to see the Marquis standing by the door. In a conservatively cut dark suit he looked part of the establishment and it was difficult to see him roughing it.

'I'm glad,' she said simply. 'This isn't a bit like Africa.'

'This isn't Africa. You need to get away from the cities to see the real country and meet the real people.'

'I'm looking forward to that.'

'It would mean too much travelling for my grandmother. When I said the real Africa I was not only thinking of the Kruger Park. That's pretty civilised too— the part where people live, I mean.' He saw her look of disappointment and smiled. 'Perhaps I should have booked you into a caravan instead of a safari lodge.'

'Is that where we're staying—in a safari lodge?'

'Yes.'

'Yorke!' an imperious voice called. 'Come in here, I want to talk to you.'

Inclining his head at Beth, he stepped back and closed the door after him.

Alone at last, Beth washed and made herself tidy, then, reluctant to interrupt the Marchioness while she was talking to her grandson, yet not knowing whether she was wanted, she went into the sitting-room. The door of the Marchioness's bedroom was closed and though she heard voices, she could not decipher the conversation. Deciding she had time to change after all, she went back to the bedroom and slipped into something cooler—a beige linen suit piped in apricot silk, with a matching apricot blouse. It was the Marchioness's choice again and showed an unerring eye for colour, since it was one that Beth would never have chosen for herself, believing beige to be incompatible with her pale skin and mousy hair. Yet it was exactly the same colour as her hair and made one notice its silvery sheen, instead of its mousy hue. She applied a generous coating of apricot lipstick to her mouth, more out of bravado than because she felt she needed to, then returned to the sitting-room. As she did so Yorke Powys came out of his grandmother's room.

'Ready?' he asked. 'Then we can go.'

'Shouldn't I stay here in case I'm needed?'

'My grandmother is asleep. I'll leave word at the desk for one of the maids to look in on her from time to time.'

'I still think I should stay here,' she protested.

'She'll be annoyed if you do.'

He walked into the corridor and Beth did the same.

'You don't need to be my guide,' she said quickly. 'I can easily go on a sightseeing tour by myself. After all, there's no language barrier here.'

His smile showed white teeth which looked even whiter against the darkness of his skin. 'I'm sure you can manage on your own, Miss Miller, but I'm equally sure my grandmother would not like it if I allowed you to do so.'

More convinced than ever that he was fulfilling a duty, Beth followed him out of the hotel to where a chauffeur-driven car was waiting for them.

For the next few hours they drove round the city, which she found disappointingly like any other city, despite the visible signs of ancient mines—huge mounds of earth which disfigured the horizon and stood as solid indication of the gold on which Johannesburg and the Union of South African had been built.

'I always think it a pity for visitors to see Johannesburg first,' the man beside her remarked. 'One should arrive in Africa via Cape Town. The sight of Table Mountain is something one doesn't easily forget.'

'Will we be going there?'

He shrugged. 'It isn't a trip you can do in a day. Even flying, it would need three days at least.'

'Spaces are so immense here,' she sighed.

'This is an immense country, Miss Miller. The only thing small about it is the population.'

'It looks very crowded to me,' she said as they came to a grinding halt in a complex of traffic.

'That's because you're in a busy city. Once you're driving in the veldt, you can go for hundreds of miles without seeing another car. You'll see that for yourself tomorrow.'

'By air?' she smiled.

'I was forgetting. Still, you'll be able to get a bird's eye view of things.' She gave a little shiver and he glanced at her. 'You can't be cold in this heat!'

'It's excitement,' she apologised. 'It always makes me shiver.'

His glance rested on her and she coloured and wished she did not find his look so disturbing.

'My grandmother wrote and said she had found a new companion, but I hadn't realised it was one as young as you.'

'I'm twenty-five,' she told him.

'You look considerably younger. I suppose it's because you are thin and pale.'

The remark was less than flattering and she was chilled by it, then chided herself for expecting him to be anything other than truthful. Besides, he was a doctor and probably saw her through medical eyes.

'I think your grandmother is quite pleased with me. She wouldn't let me stay with her otherwise.'

'I was not being critical,' he replied. 'She has sent me several letters extolling your virtues, not the least of them being your appreciation of Powys.'

'I love the house. It's the most beautiful place I've ever seen. It has an atmosphere that——' She stopped apologetically. 'But I don't need to explain Powys to you.'

His shoulders lifted slightly. 'To me it has always been a burden.'

'Always?' she ventured.

'For a long while.' He turned away from her and Beth knew he was remembering the reasons why he had left Powys in the first place. But at that time he had only planned to be absent for two years, and had the girl he loved been willing to come with him, he would no doubt have returned to England and be living in his home now, watching his children playing on those rolling green lawns. The taxi stopped and with a pang of regret she saw they were outside the hotel.

'I suggest you have a rest,' he said. 'I've booked a table in the restaurant for eight o'clock.'

'I'm glad you've made it early,' she replied. 'I encourage the Marchioness to be in bed by ten.'

'Most people eat early here,' he explained, and feeling she had said the wrong thing, she left him and went towards the lift.

He had an odd way of making her feel gauche, and even during dinner when he was politely attentive to her needs, she still had the impression he was looking at her as though from a distance. She wondered whether he felt her to be in the way and if she should have suggested having dinner in her room. Yet if the Marchioness had wanted to talk to her grandson alone, she would have said so herself, and Beth swallowed her discomfort and stared down at her plate or across to the far end of the dining room in an effort not to meet Yorke Powys's dark gaze. It was shortly after nine when he escorted them back to their suite, ignoring his grandmother's protests that she wished to stay up longer.

'You have an exhausting day ahead of you,' he overrode her demands, 'and you need to rest.'

'I won't have you treat me like an old woman.'

'Then stop behaving like one!'

The Marchioness snorted but looked humorous, and Beth filed it for future reference. The grandson might get away with a stronger hand than a companion, but a little show of strength might not come amiss. Alone in her bedroom at last, she undressed and went to sit by the window. She was too keyed up to sleep—her mind too full of new impressions—and for more than an hour she remained staring out at the brilliantly lit skyscrapers. People might dine early here, but they did not go to bed early, and even at ten o'clock there were many cars to be heard. But by midnight all was quiet, and she drew the curtains to shut out the brilliant neon lights and lay in the darkness, reminding herself that she was in South Africa with a wonderful holiday ahead. If only it did not prove to be a disappointing one for the Marchioness. Somehow she thought it would be, and felt her own pleasure tinged by sadness. Powys needed a master, but David Cecil Edward Thomas Yorke had no intention of accepting the mantle.

CHAPTER THREE

FLYING in a small plane gave one a much greater sense of being airborne than flying in a jet, and for the first few moments after lift-off Beth found it impossible to relax. But as she grew accustomed to the greater sense of motion—for the aircraft responded to every breeze—she found it enjoyable and, had it not been for the constant noise of the engines, could have believed herself to be a bird winging her way across the luxuriant continent. Seeing it from the air she realised how vast South Africa was, and could understand why Yorke Powys had said the country was underpopulated.

She had breakfasted with the Marchioness in their suite, and was sipping her coffee when the Marquis had come to collect them, treating his grandmother with the same solicitude as the night before. She had found herself surprised by it, for she had not expected him to display such a warm affection. But warm though it was, it was not warm enough to dissuade him from his determination to remain miles away from his rightful heritage. This morning his clothes were more casual: a light weight suit in a grey that matched her own linen dress, whose high neckline was marked by a demure white ruffled collar.

'Don't you think Beth is pretty?' the Marchioness had asked him with a surprising lack of finesse.

'Beauty surrounds itself with beauty,' he replied, and despite her embarrassment Beth gave him full marks for his answer.

But she had sensed him watching her as they went down in the lift, and had been consciously aware of herself and her body in a way she had never experienced before and which she put down to still being tired after the long flight. Yet she did not feel tired. She felt bright and ready for anything the world had to offer. During the journey to the airport she was told something about the Kruger and learned that it covered an area of some two million hectares and was a sanctuary for some quarter of a million antelope, several thousand African elephants and an assortment of giraffe, zebra, warthog, jackal, lion, leopard, cheetah and wild dog.

'I hope you have a camera with you,' Yorke Powys broke into Beth's thoughts, speaking loudly to make himself heard above the noise of the engines, and she shook her head to indicate no. It was difficult to tell him—when she was wearing such obviously new and expensive clothes—that she did not have money to spare to buy a camera, for though she received a generous salary, she wanted to save as much of it as possible, there being in the back of her mind the hope that one day she might use it to help her train for a degree.

But what would this elegant-looking man know of the difficulties of making ends meet? He had been born with a silver spoon in his mouth—a diamond one, she amended—and could have no conception of how the ordinary person lived. Even as she thought this she knew she was doing him an injustice, for his work alone must bring him into contact with a sufficiently wide range of people and give him some understanding of what financial problems could mean. In fact he had a few of his own, she remembered now, since one of his reasons for not wanting to maintain Powys was because he preferred to put the money into further research work. But whereas she was concerned with saving pennies, he was concerned with saving thousands of pounds, and the thought caused the corners of her mouth to lift, so that the man watching her saw it and was intrigued. A pretty little thing, he decided. Quiet and gentle as a doe, and with the same look in her eyes: large and trusting yet with fear hidden in their depths. Had life treated her badly that she should look so afraid, or was it a natural temerity? His grandmother began to question him and he turned to answer, forgetting Beth as he did so.

At noon they began to descend to the small airstrip and Beth glimpsed hundreds of impala running away from the noise, golden brown streaks against the bronze and green of a land shot through with the silver of pampas grass, which shimmered like water in the rush of air generated by the aircraft. A land rover was there to meet them, the driver a black-skinned African in a khaki uniform that indicated he worked for the Government.

'Why aren't we staying with you at the research centre?' the Marchioness wanted to know.

'Because there isn't sufficient room.'

'I thought all the doctors had their own apartments?'

'As I'm a bachelor my quarters would not be large enough for you and Miss Miller. You'll be more comfortable in a proper camp. There will be people to talk to and——'

'I came to be with *you*.'

'I'm not on leave, Grandmother. I have my work to do.'

'Tosh! For the money they pay you, you can take time off when you want.'

He smiled and shook his head, but the set of his mouth indicated annoyance and Beth knew his mild manner hid a will as inflexible as that of his grandmother. She was more than ever convinced that if they had made this journey to try to persuade him to return to England, then it was a wasted one, and she hoped the Marchioness would accept her defeat gracefully and not refuse to face up to it. What a pity a compromise could not be reached. Surely Yorke Powys knew his grandmother did not have many more years to live? Couldn't he make an effort to do as she wished for the inevitably short time left to her? For the first time she wondered if this wide-shouldered, slim-hipped man was the last male in his line or if there were a cousin who would come forward and save Powys and all it stood for? Yet this could only be done if Yorke Powys himself was dead. The thought made her gasp and he heard the sound and turned his head in her direction.

'Is anything wrong?'

'No. I—it was an insect,' she lied.

'A mosquito perhaps. Are you one of the sufferers?'

'Sufferers?'

'Some people attract them,' he explained.

'I don't know if I do. I've never encountered them before.'

'Beth is a real country bumpkin,' the Marchioness said. 'That is why I like having her with me. She is so delighted with everything that it makes me feel a generous benefactor.'

'You love that, don't you?' Yorke teased.

'You never give me the chance of being generous to you.'

'We need a mass of new equipment,' he said at once.

'That isn't the kind of generosity I mean.'

'I know,' he said dryly. 'You only like to give if you get something in return—my freedom.'

'You talk as if I want to turn you into a slave,' the

Marchioness said, 'when all I wish is for you to accept your responsibilities.'

'I have no responsibility to bricks and mortar. My responsibility is to curing disease.'

He made no attempt to hide his anger and his manner was as sharp as the glitter in his eyes. The Marchioness looked angry too and the colour came and went in her face.

'Isn't that a lodge?' Beth intervened hastily. 'I think we've arrived.'

'So we have,' Yorke said as the land rover slowed down to drive through a pair of open gates.

Mandama Safari Lodge was unlike anything Beth had anticipated, being a series of small, round white-walled cottages, each one topped with a thatched, conical-shaped roof. These were centred at random round a low building which housed the dining hall and lounge. To one side of it was another building which housed a supermarket where, she was to discover later, one could buy anything from a packet of soap flakes to an elephant door-stop. The entire area was surrounded by a six foot high wooden fence, and she stared at it in surprise.

'It's to stop the animals from jumping in and the humans from jumping out!' Yorke Powys said beside her.

'Honestly?'

'Honestly. The gates are closed at dusk each night and from then until dawn you can't get out.'

'You make it seem like a prison!'

'You'll be glad of the locked gates when you hear the animals howling,' he drawled. 'You won't even find a gamekeeper wandering round the Kruger at night. This isn't a zoo, Miss Miller, with all the animals tucked up nicely in cages. Here, it's the humans that are locked up—for their own safety—and the animals who are allowed to wander free!'

The land rover stopped outside one of the round white huts and the Marquis jumped out.

'This is your rondavel,' he said with a slight smile. 'It's a Western version of a Bantu hut. The Bantu is a generic term given to all black South Africans, but in fact they comprise many different tribes.'

'Beth knows a great deal about South Africa,' the Marchioness came into the conversation. 'When she knew we were coming here she went to Plymouth and came back armed with books.'

'As practical as she looks,' the Marquis said lightly, a remark which seemed to displease his grandmother, who gave one of her usual snorts and stalked into the rondavel.

Beth followed quickly, determined to prove she was practical by taking charge of the situation and deciding which one of the two bedrooms should be occupied by herself. Though the rondavel looked small from the outside, its interior was surprisingly large and there were two bedrooms and a well-equipped batheroom. Floral-patterned curtains hung at the windows and hand-woven rugs scattered the polished tile floor.

'You have air-conditioning,' Yorke Powys said, coming in, 'and all the windows are netted to keep out insects. But don't open the windows if you're using the air-conditioning.'

'Yes, Lord Powys,' Beth said primly, and received an old-fashioned look in return.

'I don't use my title, Miss Miller. I'm Doctor Yorke Powys and I would just as soon you called me Yorke.'

Colour washed into her cheeks and she wished she did not blush so easily. 'You m-must call me Beth,' she stammered.

'Is that your full name?'

'No. It's Elizabeth.' Conscious of the Marchioness in the other bedroom, Beth went to the door. 'Do you have any plans for us at the moment?' she asked over her shoulder.

'I thought you would have lunch and spend the heat of the day resting, then take a short drive about four o'clock. Don't expect to see much wild life, though. The best time for that is either early morning or at dusk.'

'And preferably where there's water.'

'Ah yes, I was forgetting all those books you've been reading. Are you always so assiduous in learning about a country before you visit it?'

'This is the first country I have visited properly,' she said. 'Unless you count a school holiday in Switzerland?'

His dark brows rose. 'All navy knickers and gym slips? What a horror!'

She smiled. 'Now perhaps you can appreciate why I was so excited at coming here.'

He did not answer and she wasn't sure if this indicated agreement or merely boredom with the conversation. For all the fact that he was easy to talk to, there was an underlying reserve about him that always made her feel he was only giving them half his attention, and that his mind was really preoccupied with other things which he considered more important. She wished she knew more about his work and would have liked to ask him exactly what he did and what had prompted him to take up his research. But she was afraid he might resent being questioned and could easily see him withdrawing into himself, like a snail into its shell. 'More likely a lobster than a snail,' she thought, for she felt him to be capable of snapping, were his temper aroused.

'Now what are you smiling about?' he asked.

'Was I?' she said in surprise.

'You have a disconcerting habit of lapsing into silence and then smiling. I can't make up my mind whether it's because you find the situation amusing or whether you are concerned solely with your own thoughs.'

'Sometimes it's a bit of both,' she confessed, 'but generally the situation leads me to think of something and——' she hesitated—'I have an awful habit of letting my imagination run wild.'

'You look the romantic type,' he observed.

'I thought you considered me prim and proper?'

'Prim and proper romantic!'

She laughed and the sound seemed to please him, for he smiled too. 'I'm glad you work for my grandmother. I worry about her being alone in that great big house.'

Beth forbore to say it was a worry he could avoid by returning to England, but she knew it was not her business to make such a comment.

'I will go and see about your table in the dining-room,' he continued, 'and then I want to put in a call to the research station.'

'Will we be allowed to visit there?'

'There's nothing to see except laboratories and animals.'

'In cages?' she ventured.

'Unfortunately in cages.' As though he guessed her thoughts his brows closed together. 'We do not kill animals for our research work, but if they are ill or dying we are allowed to study them. Once they *are* dead we can use them, of course.'

She was on the verge of asking him what he did, when he turned and swung out, and she went into the Marchioness's bedroom to do her unpacking. The Marchioness was lying on the bed, the only concession to her age, but even here she was sitting upright and she watched Beth with the bright black gaze of a bird.

'What do you think of Yorke?' she asked.

'He seems charming.'

'He's too obstinate.'

'A family characteristic,' said Beth dryly.

'He has the family looks too. Handsome, isn't he?'

'Yes,' Beth said, and busied herself hanging up some dresses in the wardrobe.

'Women have always been crazy about him,' the Marchioness continued. 'Why he still nurses a broken heart for Anne is something I have never fathomed.'

'He must have loved her deeply.'

'Love is a plant,' the Marchioness grunted. 'If it isn't nourished it dies, and Yorke's should have died years ago.'

'Real love doesn't always die easily,' Beth said, setting out a silver brush and comb on the dressing table.

'Are you speaking from experience?'

'I haven't been in love the way you mean, but I understand about loving someone. I saw it with my parents. My father continued to love my mother even after she had died.'

'That's quite different. It was a love based on good memories and years of happy association. What has Yorke got to remember except a few months of kiss and cuddle in the conservatory?'

Beth kept her face hidden in the wardrobe. 'I thought they grew up together?'

'So they did, but Anne was at boarding school for years and Yorke only saw her during the holidays. Then she travelled round Europe and only came home to settle on her twenty-first birthday. Three months later, they were engaged.'

'How long ago was that?'

'Five years. And he's been sour ever since.'

'He doesn't seem particularly sour to me,' Beth said mildly. 'I mean, he doesn't strike me as being a woman-hater.'

'He is not on the defensive with *you*.'

Beth carefully closed the wardrobe door and wondered why the words should hurt her so much.

'I am not insulting you, my dear,' the Marchioness said, surprising Beth by being aware of her reaction. 'I was paying you a compliment.'

'By saying your grandson doesn't see me as a woman?'

'By saying he feels at ease with you. And you cannot complain that he is treating you like a man! No, he is aware of you, but he trusts you.'

'Because he thinks I'm an ideal companion for you,' Beth said with a slight smile.

'So you are.'

Beth closed the empty case and slid it under the bed. 'I suggest we have an early lunch and then come back for a rest.'

'For one moment I thought you were going to suggest I have lunch in bed.'

'Temper would raise your blood pressure even more!'

The Marchioness chuckled and, standing up, tapped her cane on the floor as if marshalling her thoughts. 'Come, child, I'm hungry.'

Yorke was waiting for them at the entrance to the dining room.

It was crowded and there was a preponderance of children who all seemed extremely well behaved.

'It's the Boer influence,' Yorke explained when she mentioned it. 'There's a lot to be said for the way they bring up their young.'

'There's a lot to be said against them too.'

'I refuse to have any political arguments during lunchtime—or any other time either. It only leads to profitless argument.'

'Isn't it equally profitless to bury one's head in the sand?'

His eyes glinted. 'Prim, proper and now politically minded! It's too much of a combination.'

'Do you prefer women who are dumb?' she asked.

'Compliant,' he corrected. 'That's not quite the same.'

'You have to be dumb to be compliant,' he retorted, but he refused to be drawn and merely waved his spoon at her to indicate she should eat her papaya.

She did so and found it delicious, particularly when liberally sprinkled with lime juice. The rest of the lunch was equally good; chicken with a sweet and sour sauce, roast potatoes and vegetables and a large bowl of salad, followed by ice cream and fresh fruit. It was this last part of the meal that was unusually disappointing, for the apples were tasteless and the oranges dry.

'The best of South African fruit is exported,' Yorke said, peeling himself a banana. 'But you will find wonderful avocadoes here and an excellent selection of tropical fruits.' He signalled to the waiter, black as all the waiters were, and a moment later a slice of fresh pineapple was set in front of her.

Touched at Yorke's solicitude, Beth sampled it. 'It's the nicest I ever had.'

'Because it was probably picked a few hours ago. You will find the bananas equally good. The ones that are sent abroad are picked green and left to ripen in the ship or warehouse, but here you can leave them to ripen on the trees and then pick them and eat them within minutes.'

'I'd love to see bananas growing.'

'Perhaps we can arrange a tour for you. You might enjoy a drive from here to Durban.' He looked at his grandmother. 'I don't advise it for you. It would be too tiring.'

'I have no intention of going. But there is no reason why you cannot take Beth.'

'She won't need me,' came the casual reply. 'There are tours going every day. It's just a question of getting booked on one.' He looked at Beth again. 'They are really excellent value. You travel in an air-conditioned mini-bus with a guide who speaks English and Afrikaans, and you get a good look at the country on a five-day trip, all for less than fifty pounds.'

Beth felt a tremor of fear. Fifty pounds meant nothing to the man and woman sitting opposite her, but to her it represented several weeks' work.

'The trip would come with the job,' he added, as though divining her thoughts. 'You will not be expected to pay for it.'

'I don't think I wish to leave the Marchioness for so long,' she said.

'We'll talk about it later,' her employer informed her. 'It's early days yet.'

At this remark Yorke's eyes narrowed and he fixed them upon his grandmother. 'How long are you intending to stay here?'

'Until I have talked some sense into you.'

'I see.' He paused. 'I hadn't realised you had emigrated.'

Beth hid a smile and even the Marchioness could not deny one.

'You are an obstinate man, Yorke, but I would remind you that I am obstinate too.'

44

'Then it's a good thing my work will keep us apart for a great deal of the time!'

'You mean you're running away?'

'Not deliberately,' he said. 'But I did warn you that I am not on holiday. If you had warned me you were coming I could have arranged things differently, but at the moment I'm in the middle of an experiment that cannot be left to anyone else.'

'Can't you get over in the evening?'

'Only if I can cadge a lift with one of the game wardens. As I told you, the ordinary *hoi polloi* aren't allowed to drive in the park after a certain hour.'

'I didn't think that would apply to people at the research centre.'

'It applies to everyone apart from the game wardens, and even they don't go wandering round on foot.'

A long slender finger came up to rub his chin. It was a smooth-shaven chin, Beth saw, for even though he was so dark-skinned there were no unsightly blue shadows to mar the bronze tan. 'But I think I'll be able to get over for an occasional evening to see you.'

'I should hope so!' his grandmother exploded. 'I didn't come out here to look at the lions. Really, Yorke, I insist you find us accommodation at Mandama.'

'Impossible, I'm afraid. It's your own fault for coming here in such a rush.'

The malacca cane tapped the floor sharply, always a sure sign of temper with the Marchioness, and Beth hurried delved into her bag and picked out a white pill which she passed across the table.

'You missed taking one this morning,' she said, 'and the doctor wants you to take two a day.'

'You must let my grandson see the prescription. He has far more sense than that fool of a doctor.'

45

'Doctor Burton is far from a fool,' Yorke cut in, 'and I have seen what he has prescribed for you.'

'How?'

'He keeps in touch with me.'

The reply was brief, the tone mild, but it gave Beth a strange lift of her spirits. Yorke did care about his grandmother. He would not have asked Doctor Burton to write to him otherwise. The fact that he refused to return permanently to Powys only meant that he considered his work more important than a house.

'I must leave you both.' Yorke rose to his feet. 'But I have made arrangements for you to go for a drive at four o'clock and I'll meet you later this evening.' He bent to kiss his grandmother and with a brief smile in Beth's direction strode away.

In any room the tall, sunburned man would be outstanding, for there was an easy grace about him and an air of obvious command, as if he was used to having his wishes obeyed. Was this the result of his heritage or because he had, through his own intelligence, achieved a position of authority? Beth longed to know more about his work and made up her mind to ask him the moment she could. Yet even if she knew exactly how he occupied his working hours, she felt it would give her no clue towards knowing the man himself. His real personality remained hidden behind the polite smile, the cool manner and the deep, compelling dark eyes.

CHAPTER FOUR

FOR the next few days Beth and the Marchioness were left to their own devices. Yorke had arranged for a car and driver to be at their disposal, but he himself did not put in an appearance, though he telephoned each evening to see how his grandmother had spent the day.

Expecting the Marchioness to be annoyed at being alone, Beth was surprised that she took her grandson's absence in her stride, and appeared to enjoy the leisurely trips they made through the Kruger Park.

The area was so vast they could have stayed for weeks and still not seen all of it, and though the landscape had a general overall similarity, it changed with the changing of the light and the depth of blue in the sky. Beth was never sure whether she preferred it in the early morning when the dew was still damp on the grass and the bushes and trees had a hushed waiting air, or at dusk when the horizon looked like a Turner watercolour. It was then that the trees took on their most unbelievable shapes; not the abundant leafy trees that dotted the landscape, but the sparse-leafed ones like the acacia thorn, whose weird-shaped twigs seemed to be stuck with toothpicks; and the fever tree, with its countable leaves and beige branches and trunk. During the day it looked ugly and leprous, but at night its pale contorted branches resembled the limbs of ballet dancers.

Beth never grew tired of seeing strange pictures in the fancy shapes of the trees and wondering about the animals who shaded themselves beneath them. Would they still be roaming the wilderness long after the human race had disappeared from the face of the earth? Driving across mile after mile of wild country it was easy to visualise how the world had looked a million years ago and not difficult to imagine what it might look like a million years hence, if it were not destroyed by war.

Seen in their natural setting, the animals looked different from any Beth had seen on her occasional visits to the zoo. A giraffe behind bars had none of the natural grace of one roaming free, and watching a herd of them loping along on their immensely thin, stilt-like legs, she thought they seemed like prehistoric creatures come to life, their mottled golden brown skins melting into the background of grass and bush. But it was the impalas which she loved most of all. She could have spent hours watching them gambolling at play or looking at the car with startled eyes before running madly for cover. Occasionally she glimpsed young bucks fighting, but they were playful fights with none of the hard reality that would come when two adult males clashed.

The Marchioness seemed more fond of the elephants and cackled delightedly when they glimpsed one casually knocking down a sapling or pulling a young tree out by its roots with as much ease as if it were pulling a straw from a glass. They were extremely large elephants and unlike the ones Beth had previously seen in England.

'The elephants you find in a zoo are Indian,' their guide explained. 'They are more docile and easy to train and if they do run amok the damage they can do is far less than one of these. African elephants are untrainable and are so big and strong that you would need a fortress to put them in. Yet roaming free they show no sign of bad temper nor even of their immense strength.'

'None of the animals look ferocious when you see

them in their natural setting,' Beth said.

'But they will kill you just as easily if given the chance,' the guide informed her. 'That's why visitors are forbidden to get out of their cars. If a ranger catches you, you will be fined and evacuated from the park.'

On the fourth day after their arrival the Marchioness complained of a slight headache and Beth insisted they rest in the shade of some trees on the lawn outside their hut, returning inside when the midday sun was at its hottest, and remaining there even for lunch, which she ordered to be sent across to them. It was difficult to know whether her employer's indisposition was caused by fatigue or an increase in blood pressure, and Beth debated whether or not to call in the camp doctor, eventually deciding to wait until later in the day.

But by mid-afternoon the Marchioness looked considerably better and Beth's unease lessened sufficiently for her to take a stroll around the grounds. They stretched for more than an acre, housing not only the guests but also the African staff who lived in their own quarters on the far side of the camp. Everything had to be brought in from outside and since the nearest town was some distance away, she was surprised by the relative cheapness of the prices she had seen on the menu and in the small supermarket. Apart from the rondavels, there were also communal huts where entire families could live at a much cheaper rate. There was a camping site too, though the occupants here were not allowed to take their meals in the dining room of the Safari Lodge and had to fend for themselves, which they seemed to do extremely well, if the appetising smells that wafted from the caravans at mealtimes was anything to go by.

When Beth returned to her own hut she found the Marchioness sleeping in a deck chair, and she sat quietly beside her, looking out from the cool shade to where the sun beat down fiercely on the grass. Despite having avoided its glare, she had nonetheless acquired a light tan which had also bleached her hair and given it a streaky fairness she found disquieting. The Marchioness, however, had commented on it approvingly, and had insisted that Beth stop wearing her hair drawn away from her face and let it hang loose to her shoulders. It was a style Beth personally considered too young for someone no longer on the sunny side of twenty, but the older woman had laughed at her protestations, saying that if she thought like an old maid, she would become one.

'I'm one already!'

'Stuff and nonsense! Four days here and you already look a different person.'

'That's because of the beautiful clothes you bought me. I feel guilty every time I put them on.'

'You must stop being so grateful for everything. Show a little more spirit, child. When you first came to me you looked like a mouse and you acted like one. But now that you look so pretty, you should show a bit more sparkle.'

'A leopard can't change its spots.'

'Your coat *has* been changed!' came the reply. 'And even if you can't alter inside, at least put on an outward pretext.'

'I'm sorry you find me too docile,' Beth said, straight-faced. 'But I'm not such a mouse when I'm aroused.'

'But what arouses you? In all the time you've been with me you've never lost your temper once. And it can't be because I'm such an angel to get on with—at least not according to your predecessor.'

'It would take more than an old lady's bad temper to

rile me,' Beth grinned. 'Of course if you pulled your cat's tail or beat your dog...'

The Marchioness had chuckled. 'I must get Yorke to bring a cat with him tonight. I would like to see him strike a few sparks from you!'

'I didn't know the Marquis was coming over this evening?' Beth's heart had thumped alarmingly at the prospect and she was glad her voice sounded normal.

'He told me last night when he telephoned. Wear your red silk tonight, child.'

'Isn't it a bit too dressed up for here?' Beth had asked doubtfully.

'You are not wearing it for here; you are wearing it for my grandson and myself.'

'I don't think your grandson notices what I wear.'

'Young men always notice what a pretty woman wears,' the Marchioness had rejoined.

Knowing it would be ungracious to refuse her employer's request, Beth had nodded agreement. But now, as she sat in the shade thinking of the evening ahead, she regretted her promise and felt she would look like a Christmas cracker at a summer picnic. None of the visitors dressed up in the evening, merely changing from one casual outfit to another. If she entered the dining-room in her red dress everyone would notice her. Could that be what the Marchioness wanted and, if so, why?

'I see what Yorke means about your expression.' Beth turned and saw that the dark eyes were open and fixed upon her. 'You've been frowning and smiling and frowning for the last five minutes. Having a discussion with yourself, I'll be bound.'

'Debating whether or not I should have a discussion with you,' Beth said frankly. 'I honestly think my red dress will be out of place tonight. Everyone will notice me!'

'Good. I enjoy your prettiness and I want other people to enjoy it too. Be more heavy-handed with your make-up too, you have a tendency to look like a blur!'

'Who else is coming to dinner?' Beth asked suspiciously, wondering whether the Marchioness had any match-making plans.

'Only my grandson.'

The reply allayed Beth's fears and she setted back more comfortably in her chair. The movement brought her face to face with her employer who, caught off guard, had such a look of anticipation on her face that Beth was again suspicious of the woman's behaviour. But if the Marchioness was indeed match-making, whom did she have in mind? A sudden thought struck her and her hands grew clammy. Surely it couldn't be Yorke? How furious he would be if he knew. As for herself … Anger was so strong in her that she was almost prompted to speak, restrained from doing so only because she did not wish to arouse the Marchioness's blood pressure by arguing with her. Besides, the best way of dissuading her was to pretend ignorance of the plan and then, by virtue of one's behaviour, let her see she was wasting her time.

Had Yorke guessed his grandmother's intentions and was this the reason he had left them alone as soon as they had settled in here? Somehow she could not see him being overcome with embarassment at the prospect of having a paid companion foisted on to him. He was far too used to having girls thrown at his head. On looks alone he would warrant such action, and if to this one added his title and his money …

'I'm going for a walk,' she announced, and jumped up.

'You've just had one.'

Without replying, Beth hurried away, anxious to be alone and let her thoughts run free without fear of being watched. As her embarrassment lessened she felt a little gratification at the idea of the Marchioness wishing to encourage a romance between her companion and her grandson. But the gratification died as she wondered if she were merely being used as a decoy to arouse Yorke Powys's emotions sufficiently to bring him back to England in pursuit of her. Once there, his grandmother could possibly be banking on the hope that, surrounded by girls of his own class, he would see Beth for the innocent she was and turn to someone more suitable. Yes, that must be the plan. She was being used as bait.

Having satisfied herself on this point, Beth returned to the hut, debating whether or not to let Yorke know of his grandmother's ploy or to wait and see how the evening went. If he showed any sign of realising what was going on—and she would know just by looking out for the glint in his eye—then she would seek him alone and make it quite clear that she knew what game was being played and had no intention of being made one of the participants, except as a pretence in order to placate the Marchioness. If, on the other hand, Yorke appeared unaware of what was happening, then she would tackle the Marchioness herself and insist that no further attempt was made at throwing her at Yorke's head.

Having satisfied herself as to her course of action, she regarded the red dress as being a theatrical costume worn to play a part, and even saw her instructions to wear more make-up as a part of the act too. But no amount of make-up could make her look sophisticated. The bright lipstick emphasised the childishly soft con-

53

tours of her mouth and her long black lashes—spiked with mascara—stuck out stiff and straight like those of a doll, giving her eyes even more of a wide-eyed look than normal. She did not see that the incongruity of sophistication and innocence held unexpected allure, nor did she know quite what the cunningly cut dress did for the lissom lines of her figure. She only saw with satisfaction that the material closely covered her entire body and did not have the experience to know that covered curves were more enticing than exposed ones.

She went in to the Marchioness, who looked regal in beige lace, with several rows of pearls around her throat. They were the only jewels she had brought with her on the journey and she indicated Beth to fasten the safety catch for her.

'My arms are too rheumaticky to do it myself,' she explained.

Beth fastened the clasp and stepped back. 'You should wear your pearls all the time. They're beautiful.'

'I don't like old women wearing jewellery. I only put these on to stop them discolouring. Pearls lose their lustre if they're not worn.'

'Not the pearls I have,' Beth chuckled. 'They're Woolworth's special!'

'When you are young you don't need jewellery to enhance you.'

'And when you are old you shouldn't wear it!' Beth reminded her. 'So what's the point of having it?'

'Pride of possession,' came the cackle. 'That's the only reason why a woman needs jewellery. It's a man's way of showing his love.'

'Receiving jewellery wouldn't signify love to me,' Beth said quietly.

'You aren't the usual sort of girl. That's why I ...

Come along, child, we don't want to keep Yorke waiting.'

Pretending to be unaware of the unfinished sentence, Beth guided the Marchioness across the well-lit path to the dining hall. As they crossed the flagstoned courtyard, the tall figure of a man came forward to greet them and Beth hung back, strangely reluctant to let Yorke see her. But there was no way to avoid it and bracing her shoulders she resumed walking.

Yorke lifted his grandmother's hands to his lips. It was a gesture that went well with his appearance, for in dark trousers and a white linen jacket, he looked every inch a Spanish grandee. It was only as he straightened and the Marchioness moved out of the way that he had his first full glimpse of Beth who, framed in the harsh white light of the dining-room entrance, glowed like a slim red candle. For an instant there was a look of stupefaction on his dark face, then it became urbane once more, though there was a glint in his eyes that made her feel uneasy.

'Well, well,' he drawled. 'The yellow tea rose has become a scarlet geranium.'

'Surely you can do better than that,' the Marchioness exclaimed.

'I thought Beth would appreciate being likened to a flower.' He flashed Beth a look that belied his words and her unease grew. 'Do you object to being called a geranium?'

'The word "scarlet" has various meanings,' she replied quietly.

'I'm sure you know which one applies to you.'

Determined not to show her dismay at his reaction to her—it was considerably more antipathetic than she had anticipated—she did not answer him, and followed silently as he settled them at a table and chairs set out underneath the trees. A small yellow light glowed nearby, giving off a vapour to keep away the insects, and it robbed Beth's dress of redness and made them all look like lemon ghosts.

'What will you have?' he asked Beth.

'Orange juice.'

'It doesn't go with the dress.'

Convinced by now that he was furious with her, she again remained silent, and he snapped his fingers to attract the attention of a waiter and ordered a sherry, and a Bloody Mary and a whisky. When it came she knew better than to argue and sipped the red drink as though she liked the taste.

'Well,' he asked softly, leaning towards her, 'aren't you angry with me for ordering you something you didn't want?'

'You obviously feel the need to vent your temper on someone.'

'And of course you know why?'

'Don't you think Beth looks well?' the Marchioness cut in.

'Extremely so. And so do you.'

'Because I had a long rest today.'

'Weren't you well?' He was instantly alert and though he spoke to his grandmother, he looked at Beth. She shook her head imperceptibly and he nodded and went back to sipping his drink.

At dinner he spoke little, seemingly preoccupied with inner thoughts. The Marchioness ignored his silence and determinedly included him in the conversation even when he did not answer. Only when coffee was served did he come out of his reverie, though he again ignored Beth and only spoke to her when forced to do so.

'When will you be able to spend some time with us?' the Marchioness asked him.

'I don't know. I'm working on several experiments and by the time I'm free, you will have returned home.'

'I have not booked our return flights yet.'

'How long do you intend staying?'

'That depends on you.'

'No, Grandmother,' he said gently, 'it depends on *you*. I intend to stay here indefinitely.'

'How obstinate you are!' The words exploded forth. 'You can't spend the rest of your life in a jungle!'

'I would hardly call Mandama a jungle.'

'You know very well what I mean.'

'I wish you knew equally well what *I* mean.' He was still speaking gently, but there was no doubting the inflexibility of his expression. 'I suggest we drop the subject. I'm sure it's embarrassing for Beth.'

'Beth knows exactly how I feel. She has heard me talk about you often enough. How much longer are you going to let Anne keep you away from your inheritance?'

Yorke's chair scraped violently back as he stood up, but his voice remained gentle. 'I suggest we go and sit in the lounge.'

Only heightened colour gave indication of the Marchioness's awareness that she had incurred her grandson's wrath, for she said nothing to Beth and took her arm in silence, leaning heavily on it as they went into the long narrow room where people could sit and stare out at the lamplit grass. It was as warm tonight as it had been during the day, with a heaviness in the air that indicated a storm. Even the animals were restless, for an occasional shrill cry was heard that set Beth's nerves tingling.

Yorke was once more in complete control of himself, though as fresh coffee was set before them, he surprisingly returned to the subject which, a moment before, had nearly precipitated an argument.

'You and I will have to have a chat before you return home, Grandmother. I know why you came out here and I was hoping you would return without my having to be brutally frank.'

'You have always been brutally frank.'

'But you have never believed me.'

'Because I cannot believe you mean to make Africa your home.'

'I have never said I wouldn't return to England. Merely that I cannot see myself returning to Powys. What would I do with a house that size?'

'Raise a family.'

'Of little Powys bastards? Come, Grandmother, you don't mean that!'

'I assume you would take a wife first.' Red spots of colour mottled the wrinkled cheeks, but the voice was as incisive as ever. 'How much longer are you going to let Anne ruin your life?'

'It has nothing to do with Anne,' he said curtly.

'I think I'll go to my room,' Beth murmured, but as she made to stand, Yorke shook his head.

'You have already done your damage so you might as well stay.'

'What damage?' she asked, startled by his comment.

'Made yourself look——'

'Yorke!' The Marchioness's voice held such autocratic command that the man obeyed it instinctively. 'You have no right to blame Beth. I am the one with whom you should be angry. I think you know that well enough.'

'Yes,' he said quietly, 'I think I do. It's just that I never expected such behaviour from you. You have always been more subtle.'

'Where has subtlety got me?'

He gave a deep sigh and rubbed a clenched hand across his forehead. 'If only I could make you understand that nothing you can do will make any difference. I have a career ... work that I love ... I have no intention of giving it up to become a titled landowner.'

'But you *are* a titled landowner!'

'I won't be if I have my way. You know I want to give Powys to the National Trust.'

'And what about all the people on the estate? Families who have depended on us for generations? Who have farmed your land——'

'I will give them their farms.'

'It will cost you a fortune in taxes. I thought you wanted to use your money for research?'

'I will use what's left.'

'Have you no sense of duty?' the old lady whispered. 'Can you turn your back on everything your family have cherished for centuries?'

'Let us say I have a different sense of duty.'

'To sick animals?'

'To sick people. The research we do here has already benefited human beings.'

'Why can't you do the same work in England?' she demanded.

'Because there aren't enough facilities.'

'Then build your own research laboratory.'

'It would cost more than a million pounds to set it up.'

'Is there nothing I can say to make you change your mind?'

'No,' he said quietly. 'We would both be a great deal happier if you could accept that.'

'I will never accept it as long as there is breath in my body.' The tall, thin figure got to its feet, trembling slightly though the cane remained firm on the ground. 'I will go to my room alone,' she said as Beth and Yorke rose with her. 'Please remain where you are.'

She turned and walked out, though Yorke did not resume his seat until she had disappeared through the door. Then with a heavy sigh he sat down, and though Beth longed to walk out too, she lacked the courage to do so.

'What is your opinion of all this?' he asked abruptly. 'Don't bother being tactful—just truthful.'

'I don't know enough about the situation to give an opinion.' She hesitated. 'Why have you been rude to me this evening?'

It was his turn to hesitate. 'I hate red.' There was a longer hesitation before he added: 'It was my ex-fiancée's favourite colour.'

Mortification kept Beth silent. How could the Marchioness have chosen this dress for her and encouraged her to wear it tonight? Had she deliberately wanted to remind her grandson of the long departed but still haunt-ingly pervasive Anne? And what had she hoped to gain by it? To make him see perhaps that one girl in red was very much like another? If this had been her in-tention she had failed dismally, for the sight of Beth in a red dress had roused him to fury, and had probably made him realise yet again that no one could approxi-mate the woman for whom he still hungered.

'I'm not remaining in Africa because I'm still heart-sick,' he said suddenly. 'Though I know my grandmother would have you believe it.'

'Only because she thinks it's true.'

'Well, it isn't. In the beginning it was, but not now. I stay here because I love the work and because I can't do it anywhere else.'

'Only in a little research station stuck in the middle of the Kruger Park?'

His smile was dry. 'You're wrong in your assessment of Mandama. Small it may be, but it has a big reputation. Research workers come here from all over the world.'

'I'm sorry,' she apologised. 'I shouldn't have spoken.'

'I have never known ignorance keep a woman silent.'

She chuckled and his dark look of anger decreased. 'You have a nice laugh, Beth. It's different from the way you look.'

'Oh?' She was curious. 'What sort of laugh is it?'

'Warm and intriguing.'

'Meaning that I'm——'

'Cool and controlled,' he interrupted. 'At least that's the first impression you have, though now I'm not so sure.'

'Don't let my fine feathers fool you.'

'They haven't. They've merely helped me to see below the mask you wear. Perhaps you are a tropical flower that needed the sunshine in order to blossom.'

'I'll soon fade into insignificance when I return to England!' she said tartly, rising to her feet. 'If you'll excuse me. I will go to bed. Are you returning to Mandama tonight?'

'No. I'm staying here. I thought I would take you for a drive tomorrow.'

'You should have told your grandmother. She'll be delighted.'

'It's the least I can do,' he sighed. 'I feel I have let her down in every other way.'

'If you believe you are doing what is right, you have no need to feel guilty.'

He shrugged and walked beside her along the footpath that led to the rondavels.

'I am trained as a doctor and I am engaged in what I believe to be valuable medical research,' he said as though reciting something he had said to himself many times before. 'I don't want to waste my life showing visitors round my stately home or having farmers touch their forelocks to me as I go past. If it were possible I would like nothing better than to keep Powys, but unfortunately I can't see any way of doing so. Grandmother is old and when she dies there will be no one to live in the house. That's why I want to give it to the National Trust. I would rather have it become a museum than stand empty and rot.' He was silent for a moment before speaking again. 'It was my determination to do research work at Mandama that made my fiancée leave me, yet my grandmother still thinks she can succeed where Anne failed.'

'Perhaps she is hoping you regret what you did,' Beth said softly.

'The past can't be changed,' he replied, 'and to regret it is pointless.'

'But do you regret it?' she asked, and then realising how personal a question it was, said quickly: 'Please forgive me for saying that; I don't mean to pry.'

'I'm sure you don't.' His voice was friendlier than it had been all evening. 'But for heaven's sake try and make my grandmother accept the position. She is fond of you, Beth, and she might listen to what you say.'

'She can only hear the heartbeat of Powys,' Beth said huskily, 'and she will do everything to keep it alive.'

'It will die,' he said with finality. 'I am the last of the line.'

She shivered and put her hand on his arm without knowing she had done it. She felt its sinewy strength beneath her fingers and she dropped her hand at once. 'Don't talk like that, Yorke! It's morbid.'

'But it's the truth. When I die, so does the family name.'

Beth thought of the Long Gallery and knew a sense of anguish. 'Then marry and have children,' she cried. 'Anne isn't the only woman in the world!'

'It's taken *you* to remind me.'

She stared at him, but it was too dark to see his expression. 'I'm not very tactful, am I?' she murmured.

'These days, being tactful often means being dishonest. And I'm glad you aren't.'

They reached her hut and he put his hand on her arm. She trembled at the touch, but he appeared not to notice. 'I'll see you in the morning, Beth. Thank you for being so indulgent of my bad temper.'

'I won't wear red again.'

'It doesn't bother me now.' He waited for her to unlock the door and did not move away until she had closed it behind her.

Beth remained leaning against it until she could no longer hear his footsteps, then quietly tiptoed into her bedroom. There was no light burning in the Marchioness's room and she was careful to make as little noise as possible as she undressed and got into bed. So much had happened this evening that her thoughts were a jumble, but slowly she began to sort them out and the important ones remained on the surface of her mind like phosphorescence on the sea, changing shape and meaning as she examined them, first from one viewpoint and then from another.

What had Yorke meant by his last two remarks to her? Why did red no longer bother him when it had obviously done so earlier in the evening? And why had she served to remind him that Anne was not the only woman in the world? She did not let herself believe the obvious meaning, for therein could lie heartache. Hurriedly she reconsidered his last remark about not minding her wearing red. Was it his way of telling her he did not care what she wore, or did he mean that having recovered from the shock of seeing her in the colour he had always associated with the woman he loved, he could no longer be shocked by it? She could find so many different answers that she had no means of knowing which was the right one. Nor was she likely to know, for the more she saw of Yorke the more difficult he was to assess. Only her emotions were becoming clearer. Frighteningly clearer.

She sat up in the darkness, hugging her knees and resting her chin on them the way she had done as a child when she was worried. But she was a child no longer. She was a woman in love.

'I can't be,' she whispered. 'How can I love a man I only met a week ago?' Yet she had met him months ago when she had first come to Powys. She had met him in every single family portrait, in every line of family history she had read. Yorke was a product of his forefathers and, as such, she knew the deep emotions within him; emotions he was fighting to overcome. That was why she had felt such a strong affinity between them when she had met him at the airport, when she had sat beside him in the taxi during their tour of Johannesburg and when she had walked with him tonight in the warm darkness. Admittedly there was a great deal about Yorke Powys she did not know, but they were surface things; the real values of the man had been born in him and would remain with him till he died. Her throat contracted and she swallowed hard. For her, Yorke was already dead, for the future he planned for himself did not include loving a woman; at least not in the way she wanted love to be. He might be willing to give himself to one for a few weeks, possibly a few months, but in the long term he wanted to be alone. How deeply he must have loved the unknown Anne for it to have marked his life so disastrously. She herself would never be able to command such intensity of feeling in anyone. And a good thing too, she decided, suddenly angry at the thought of Yorke wasting all he could offer. She might be a fool, but he was an even bigger one!

CHAPTER FIVE

MAN proposes and God disposes. The proverb came to Beth's mind the next morning when the Marchioness developed a temperature which necessitated calling in the resident doctor, who examined her cheerily but spoke far less cheerily to Beth and Yorke about high blood pressure and the dangers that could result from too much sightseeing and excitement.

'But we've been very careful not to overdo things,' Beth felt duty bound to explain.

'Well, she's in a high state of tension and fatigue.'

'Her nervous condition is my fault,' Yorke said heavily. 'We quarrelled last night.'

'Worst thing in the world for her,' the doctor grunted.

'It was unavoidable, I'm afraid.'

'Maybe it was, but if you don't want her to have a stroke, try and avoid quarrelling any more.'

Yorke frowned worriedly. 'Is it all right if we move her to Mandama? Then I'd be able to keep an eye on her the whole time.'

'That would be ideal for her. By all means do so.' The doctor looked pleased. 'She'd be far more contented if she were with you, and your own camp doctor is an excellent fellow.'

'I thought you said there was nowhere for us to stay?' Beth commented.

'There isn't. I'll have to see what strings I can pull.'

Leaving him to this task, Beth went to sit with the Marchioness and when he returned an hour later, she could see from his face that he was satisfied.

'Well, Grandmother,' he said. 'If you can't win by fair means you'll try to win by foul!'

'If you think I like being confined to my bed——' his grandmother responded, her tone nowhere near as angelic as the picture she presented in a silk nightgown and frilly bedjacket.

'I'm sure you don't,' he said gently. 'Now let Beth help you into a coat and pair of slippers.'

'You aren't taking me to hospital?' There was no mistaking the fear in the dark eyes.

'I'm taking you to Mandama,' Yorke explained. 'Dr Vale—one of the biologists—has kindly offered to move out of her apartment and let you and Beth live there for a few weeks.'

The Marchioness quickly caught the feminine gender. 'You've never mentioned her in any of your letters.'

'There are many people at Mandama whom I have never mentioned. But Rowena's only been working there for the past three months.'

'Is she English?'

'Welsh,' he said, and precluded further conversation by going to the door. 'I'd like to leave as soon as possible. You won't settle down properly until we've moved you.'

He went out and Beth turned to search for the Marchioness's coat. She had wondered what her reaction would be at seeing Yorke again so soon after realising she was in love with him, but with her whole concern focused on her employer, her emotions were in limbo and Yorke was merely the man of the family on whom she could gratefully lean.

'So we're finally getting to stay at Mandama,' the Marchioness murmured as Beth wrapped her in a coat.

'If I believed in mind over matter,' Beth said dryly, 'I'd

be wondering if you deliberately sent your blood pressure soaring!'

'When I think about that grandson of mine, it goes up to flash point all by itself!'

Beth laughed, and though she knew there was some truth in the assertion, she did not feel reassured. The Marchioness looked every one of her seventy-four years and there was a tremor in her body that made it difficult for her to walk steadily. Wondering how the woman would withstand a long drive in a land rover, Beth was delighted to see a luxurious limousine waiting for them. Not only was it as well sprung as an upholstered settee, it was also air-conditioned, and within a few moments of leaving the Lodge the Marchioness fell asleep.

Afraid that any conversation would awaken her, Yorke and Beth remained quiet, and she forced herself to stare out at the passing scene and pretend she was watching for a glimpse of animals. Yet she was intensely aware of the man beside her and wished she had had the hindsight to have realised that falling in love with him was inevitable. Loving his home as she did, steeping herself in the history of his family and forming a romantic picture of him as seen through his grandmother's eyes, it was not to be wondered that she had been susceptible to him. Even old and ugly he would have attracted her, how much more inevitable it had been when he was so outrageously good-looking. There was no point pretending—even as a day-dream—that he would ever see her as anything other than his grandmother's companion. He might be friendly towards her, but it would not progress beyond that; to think otherwise was courting disaster.

Angrily she wondered why she had always found it impossible to fall in love with the young men she had met in the past, several of whom would willingly have married her. Yet her own lack of interest in them had soon killed their ardour, for she had found it impossible to pretend to a warmth she did not feel and had wondered whether being the only child of elderly parents had affected her ability to be at ease with people of her own age. And then, like a fool, she had fallen in love almost at first sight. But not with a man with whom it might have been possible to have had a relationship, but with David Cecil Edward Thomas Yorke, fifteenth Marquis of Powys.

'Look at the zebra, Beth,' Yorke said softly in her ear, and she followed his finger to see about fifty of them running in the distance, their black and white striped coats garish against the yellow green scrub.

The road on which they were travelling was a tarmac one and there were many other cars on it, most of them meandering slowly along, their occupants gazing avidly from left to right, determined not to miss a single sight of animals. Occasionally a ranger's truck went by at a faster pace, though no car dared follow suit, for it was prohibited to drive at more than twenty miles per hour in case one hit an animal crossing the road. Beth had imagined that the animals would keep as far away as they could from human beings and vehicles, and she had been astonished that this wasn't the case, for one frequently saw groups of baboons sunning themselves in the middle of the road, or glimpsed elephants ambling from one side to the other, even passing directly in the path of a car to look around them as though admiring the scenery. No wonder a speed limit had to be enforced!

'How much further do we have to go?' she whispered.

'We're nearly there.' She turned back to the window and resolutely remained in that position until they swung off the main road on to a narrower one, crossed a bridge spanning a muddy brown river and drove for another mile.

'Here we are.' Yorke touched her arm and she looked beyond the driver's shoulders at what seemed to be a replica of the Safari Lodge they had just left. There was the same high wooden fence around its buildings and the same heavy gates through which they drove. But once inside, the Mandama Research Centre could not be mistaken for any tourist rest camp, for there was an efficient bustle about the place that made one think of white jackets and stethoscopes. Not that there were any to be seen; the few men and women she glimpsed wore casual safari suits or cotton dresses.

The main building stood in the centre of a lush green lawn and though its windows were shaded by blinds, she glimpsed functional benches bristling with tubes and short-sleeved men bent over them. This was obviously the work centre and behind it stood another large building with a verandah running the length of the top floor.

'That's the married quarters used to house assistants and technicians,' Yorke said. 'The senior staff members live in rondavels.'

'Rondavels like ours?' Beth asked, avoiding looking into his eyes.

'Yes. Some are very large and have two bedrooms and a separate living room, while others have a bedroom-cum-living room. Accommodation tends to go according to rank.'

'Where do you live?' the Marchioness asked, rousing herself.

'In one of the smaller ones. That was why I didn't offer it to you in the first place.'

'How is it that Dr Vale has more room than you?'

'She shares with another woman who had to go to Cape Town for a month. That was why she was able to loan it to you.'

'It was kind of her.'

'You will have a chance to tell her so personally. She is looking forward to meeting you.'

'Is she young?'

'Under thirty,' he said without inflection.

'I can't understand any young woman wanting to stick herself out here,' the Marchioness commented, looking through the window.

'It's a far cry from Bond Street and the Burlington Arcade, but it has its compensations.'

'Only if you are husband-hunting. There is always an abundance of men in the tropics.'

He laughed and shook his head. 'Marriage is the last thing Rowena has in mind. She is a dedicated biologist—and an excellent one.'

The car stopped outside a round, whitewashed hut almost identical to the one they had earlier vacated, and Yorke escorted his grandmother into it. The interior was functional, with easy chairs covered in beige linen and striped African wool curtains and matching rugs. The two bedrooms were identical in size and the Marchioness took the first one she came to, looking surprisingly relieved to lie on the bed.

'I'll leave you to settle in,' Yorke announced, 'and go and arrange for the dining room to send over all your meals.'

'Do most people cook for themselves?' Beth asked.

'Some do, some don't. Rowena doesn't bother. She eats in the communal dining room.'

'Is that where you eat?' the Marchioness murmured.

He nodded. 'I'm not a very domestic animal, nor do I

care much about food—other than the fact that it stops me from feeling hungry.'

'You've become a Philistine!'

He refused to be baited and with a wave of his hand he left them. Within half an hour Beth had settled the Marchioness in bed and unpacked for them both. She knew it was going to be bitter-sweet to stay here, for it meant she would be seeing much more of Yorke and this would make it all the harder for her to get him out of her mind when they returned to England. Yet at least it would give her a store of memories to look back on in the years ahead. 'When I'm living alone with my cat and my parrot,' she thought, and immediately rejected the idea, for her reflection—slim and unexpectedly vital in primrose yellow cotton—looked anything but spinsterish.

'Go and explore,' the Marchioness ordered. 'I don't want you fussing around all the time.'

'I'm your companion,' Beth reminded her. 'That's the reason I'm with you.'

'It was not my reason for bringing you here.'

'I know.'

'What do you know?'

Refusing to be drawn, Beth forestalled further questions by putting on a pair of sunglasses and obeying her orders to go out and explore.

The Research Centre was far larger than she had expected. Indeed it seemed a world of its own, having a large supermarket, a bookshop, a hut signposted 'Cinema' and a dining hall and communal recreation room that vied with the Safari Lodge for attractiveness. There was also a small school, though the children in it did not appear to go beyond the age of five. Perhaps after that their parents sent them away or themselves left to work in towns. The more Beth looked around, the more she began to appreciate why Yorke had made this his life. If one were totally absorbed in one's work, it must be advantageous to spend one's spare time with people of a similar disposition. This caused her to think of Rowena Vale and she wondered if the woman was equally dedicated.

Beth rounded a corner and, coming upon some welcome shade, decided to remain here for a moment. Her sunglasses cut out the glare but they did not diminish the heat, and her fine hair clung to her temples and the nape of her neck. Taking off her sunglasses, she dabbed her handkerchief over her brow and looked round for somewhere to sit. There was no seat within sight and she leaned against the wall. She was still leaning there, not feeling ill but feeling distinctly under par when Yorke came out of a door opposite. He stopped in surprise as he saw her.

'Are you looking for me?'

'No.' Her heart started to beat so fast that she found it difficult to speak. 'I was resting in the shade. It's very hot, you know.'

'I do know,' he said distinctly, 'but I don't think you do.' He came to stand beside her, so tall and dark that she was instantly aware of how small she was and strained her shoulders to give herself an extra inch.

'You'd better come inside and have a cold drink.'

She followed him into a clinical-looking room that held laboratory benches and a large desk, and thankfully sank on to a chair, for the room was beginning to revolve around her. It was ridiculous to feel ill without any reason. It was no hotter today than it had been yesterday, but yesterday she had been heartwhole...

'Drink this.'

The rim of a glass clattered on her teeth and she opened her eyes. Yorke was holding a glass of colourless liquid and she took it from him and drank it, shuddering slightly at the bitter taste.

'You shouldn't go around without a sun hat,' he continued, and his hand came down on the top of her head, his fingers warm on her scalp. 'Such fine hair too. You'll get heat-stroke if you aren't careful.'

'I feel better now.' She went to rise, but he did not take his hand away and she subsided back on the chair, wondering what he would do if she flung her arms around his waist and buried her face against his chest. The thought made her tremble and aware of it, though fortunately unaware of the reason, he peered at her.

'Perhaps you'd better see a doctor.'

'No, no. It's just the heat and—and I suppose I'm worried about your grandmother.'

'She'll be fine once she has had a rest,' he said gently and, dropping his hand to his side, walked over to the desk.

He had taken off his jacket and through his creamy silk shirt she glimpsed the dark shadow of hairs on his chest and saw the ripple of muscles as he moved. She could think of nothing to say and was content to remain where she was and enjoy being able to watch him, wishing her eyes were camera lenses so that she could photograph him and keep him indelibly clear in her mind's eye.

'There you are, Yorke.' A firm, clear voice made Beth turn round as a girl in her late twenties came into the room.

She was taller than average—about five feet eight—with a well proportioned figure whose curves were attractively outlined by a tightly belted shirt dress. Her hair was richly black and her skin golden and she glowed with health and vitality. Without having to be told, Beth knew immediately that this was Rowena Vale.

'I came to see if you were ready for lunch,' the girl was speaking again and Yorke came round from behind his desk.

'I'm glad you came in, Rowena,' he said easily. 'I would like you to meet Beth.'

Brown eyes, several shades lighter than Yorke's, stared into Beth's grey ones, and the wide mouth curved in a smile to show strong white teeth.

'Welcome to Mandama.' Rowena Vale shook Beth's hand briskly. 'I hope you'll like it here.'

'Beth is the sort of girl who would like it anywhere,' Yorke said, and Beth would have given a great deal to know if he thought her lacking in discrimination or too easy-going.

'It seems pleasant so far,' she said firmly, 'but I'll reserve judgment until I know my way around.'

'That shouldn't take you long.' Rowena was still smiling, though her eyes remained hard and curiously lifeless. 'I don't know if Yorke has told you, but there are lots of unattached males around. You'll be a sight for sore eyes.'

'Oh no, she won't,' said Yorke. 'I'm not letting Beth loose on our wild Australians!'

Beth looked at him questioningly, but before he had a chance to explain, Rowena did so.

'We have a group of Aussies working here for six months, and they're a pretty wolfish pack.'

Beth gave the smile expected of her and stood up. 'If you're going to lunch——' she began, and was stopped by Yorke who put his hand under her elbow and walked between her and Rowena to the door.

'You must join us,' he said.

'I can't. Your grandmother——'

'Won't disappear if she's left alone for an hour. Anyway, you know she doesn't like being fussed over.'

'Where is the Marchioness?' Rowena Vale asked.

'Resting,' Yorke replied. 'I'll take you to meet her later this afternoon. She wants to thank you for giving up your quarters.'

'That's the least I can do for you.' Rowena switched the air-conditioning to boost before closing the door of the laboratory.

'It will be like an ice box when we get back,' Yorke complained.

'Much more refreshing for us!'

'And I was brought up to believe women were the weaker sex!' Yorke said plaintively.

'You know you don't believe that,' Rowena laughed, and matched her steps to his long loping ones.

Trying to keep pace with them as they made their way to the dining hall, Beth wondered if Rowena was always so smilingly in command of everything. Certainly she gave the impression of confidence: not merely by her manner, which was brusque and assertive, but by the way she carried herself. So must the Amazons have marched into battle. But what was Rowena Vale fighting for—or was it more apt to ask 'for whom'?

In the dining room the girl was greeted on all sides, which indicated that she was at least superficially popular, and took her place on Yorke's right hand as they seated themselves at a table by the window. Every gesture she made managed to convey the familiarity which existed between herself and the man, and Beth wished she had not paused for a rest outside Yorke's rooms and so been unable to avoid sharing a meal with them.

'What do you think of Africa?' Rowena asked her as iced water was set before them.

'I haven't seen enough of it to form an opinion.'

'But you've been here more than a week.' The comment seemed to convey Beth's inadequacy. 'Surely you have some idea of the way you feel about it?'

'It's an enormous country,' Beth said faintly, 'and from what I've seen so far, it's also extremely beautiful.'

Rowena glanced at Yorke, her expression amused. 'You should arrange for—er—Miss Miller to take a few more tours before going back to England. She should certainly see Cape Town and Durban, and the Garden Tour is a must.'

'Considering you've only flown to Cape Town and back,' Yorke teased, 'you're in no position to talk!'

'I came out here to work,' Rowena said calmly. 'I don't consider myself a tourist.' She picked up the menu and studied it, then gave her order to the young black boy who had come to stand beside her. She had a lovely lilting voice, Beth conceded, her Welsh birth audible through its tone rather than its accent.

'What will you have, Miss Miller?' Rowena asked. 'I can recommend the stew. At least the cook can't overdo that!'

Beth hesitated, not wanting to eat anything yet reluctant to cause a fuss by saying so.

'Beth will have consommé,' Yorke said, and looked at the boy. 'Make it a large bowl and bring some dry crackers with it. I'll have the lamb.' As the boy loped away Yorke looked at her. He gave no excuse for having ordered her lunch, but his expression told her that he knew how she felt. 'Don't pretend to feel better than you do. You aren't fooling anyone.'

'Are you ill?' Rowena asked.

'It's the heat, I think,' Beth explained.

'And a touch of tourist tum too, I should think,' Yorke said, which made Beth turn scarlet.

'Now you've embarrassed the child,' Rowena protested, shaking her head at him.

'Hardly a child at twenty-four,' he drawled.

'Really?' Brown eyes were disbelieving as they rested on Beth's slight figure and small, pointed face.

'Don't be misled by Beth's air of gentleness,' Yorke said. 'Those big grey eyes mask a sharp little brain.'

'I'm glad to hear it,' said Rowena. 'I don't have time for stupid women.'

'I understand you are a biologist?' Beth felt duty bound to contribute to the conversation, and though the question was banal, it happily gave Rowena the opportunity to say exactly what she did. Listening, it was impossible to doubt her fervour—or Yorke's too for that matter—since the conversation soon turned from Rowena's own research into the work they were doing together. From the little Beth could make out, it was concerned with a particularly virulent type of fever, the cause of which had only recently been discovered.

'I thought you were working on rabies,' Beth said to Yorke.

'I am. This new project of ours is related to it.'

'Yorke is a brilliant biologist,' Rowena stated. 'He has already made some very important discoveries.'

'You're exaggerating.' Yorke looked none too pleased. 'We work here as a team; that's the reason for our strength.'

'But some of us have greater strength than others. You know very well you——'

'My dear Rowena,' he drawled his interruption of her, 'your prejudice is showing!'

'Can you blame me?' She looked him fully in the face. She was leaning slightly towards him, her full breasts straining against the material of her dress. It was impossible not to recognise what a good-looking young woman she was, and Beth knew that the Marchioness would see it too. Would this mean that she herself would no longer be thrown at Yorke's head? After all, a talented and beautiful biologist was far more suitable bait than a nondescript little companion. All the Marchioness had to do was to fire Rowena with enthusiasm for Powys. Surreptitiously Beth glanced at Yorke. He was returning Rowena's smile, but it was impossible to guess what thoughts went on behind those dark, carefully masked eyes.

'Do you mind if I leave you both?' Yorke was pushing back his chair. 'I'd like to have coffee with my grandmother.'

'I can go and see if she's all right,' Beth said quickly.

'No. Stay where you are.'

Uncertain whether he wished to talk to the Marchioness alone, Beth obeyed him, and as he walked out of the dining room, she stared down at her coffee cup, aware of the Welsh girl watching her.

'How long have you worked for the Marchioness?' Rowena asked.

'A few months.'

'Don't you find it dull being with an old lady?'

'You wouldn't say that if you knew the Marchioness.'

Sharp teeth bit on the full red mouth. 'Sorry, Miss Miller, I wasn't being derogatory.'

'Please call me Beth,' seemed the best way of getting over the momentary flare of antagonism. 'You won't find the Marchioness dull when you meet her.'

'So Yorke said. But then he's biased. He is extremely

79

fond of his grandmother, as I'm sure you know.'

'And she adores him.'

'That much I gathered,' Rowena said dryly. 'That's why she's here, isn't it? To persuade him to give up his work and settle at Powys.' Rowena signalled for more coffee. 'What's the Castle like? Yorke never talks about it.'

'It's beautiful. Large, but it still has the quality of a real home.'

'He'll have to be coerced into returning there.' The tone was harsh. 'But I daresay the Marchioness knew that when she brought *you* here. The resemblance is staggering.' She saw Beth's look of puzzlement and gave a sharp smile. 'Don't tell me you don't know that you're the exact image of Anne!'

Beth's heart fluttered in her throat. It had been bad enough to know that when she wore red she reminded Yorke of his ex-fiancée, but to learn that she actually looked like her was embarrassing to the point of wanting to make her rush away from Mandama this very instant. With an effort she kept her control, helped by the knowledge that Rowena Vale was hoping otherwise.

'Did you know Anne?' she managed to say.

'I've seen some snaps of her. Yorke was sorting through a bundle of photographs and they fell out.' Rowena leaned her chin on her hands. 'I was astonished when I saw you,' she confessed. 'You're paler and not as poised-looking, but you could pass for her twin.'

Beth was glad her own hands were under the table, for they were visibly shaking. Many mystifying things were now becoming explicable: the Marchioness's decision to come to Africa; her determination to take Beth; the new wardrobe of clothes she had insisted on buying her and the red dress—that dreadful red dress.

Anger swept away Beth's normal placidity as she understood exactly why Yorke had been so taken aback when he had seen her in it. Yet even he had not been honest when she had asked him why he did not like her. 'Is it the dress?' she had questioned, and he had said yes, allowing her to believe it was only the colour that had disturbed him and not the fact that she had looked like a copy of the girl he wished desperately to forget.

'I'm surprised Yorke never told you that you looked like her.' Rowena was speaking again. 'When first I saw you I almost called you Anne.'

'Perhaps he didn't want me to know in case it embarrassed me.'

'I hope it hasn't. I'm sure Yorke doesn't love her, though obviously the Marchioness still thinks he does, or she wouldn't have brought you here.'

'Aren't you jumping to conclusions? After all, I'm the Marchioness's companion.'

'You may be right.' Rowena's tone belied what she was saying. 'Anyway it doesn't matter. She'll find out soon enough that she was wrong.' The vivid face looked past Beth and a bright smile widened the mouth. 'There's Yorke.'

Jumping up, Rowena went towards him.

Beth followed slowly, wishing she need not see Yorke while she was in such a state of turmoil. But obviously her face did not give away her thoughts, for he smiled easily as she came abreast of him.

'Grandmother would like you to sit with her,' he said. 'Come along and I'll walk you back.'

'I know the way, thank you.' She slipped past him, walking as quickly as she could without breaking into an actual run. But if she had hoped to avoid him she was doomed to disappointment, for he soon caught up with her, his hand on her forearm forcing her to slow down.

'Do you want to faint again?' he asked irritably.

'I didn't faint before.'

'Only because I found you in time.' He glanced at her. 'Are you annoyed with me about something?'

'No.'

'Then why did you rush off like that?'

'Because I've already taken up enough of your time.'

His face cleared. 'I suppose Rowena has been telling you how valuable our time is! You shouldn't take any notice of her. She's inclined to be obsessive about work.'

'Aren't *you*?'

Her sharpness made him glance at her and what he saw there decided him against replying. Instead his brows came together in the quick frown he frequently gave when he was taken by surprise. 'By that, I assume you are referring to my insistence on staying here?'

'Naturally.'

They were in sight of a group of rondavels and he stopped walking and blocked her path. 'I would come back to England if I could continue my work there. I'm not staying away from Powys because of a broken heart.'

'Really?'

'Really.' He caught his lower lip between his teeth. 'At one time I was—I'll admit that—but not now. Definitely not now.' He pointed ahead of him. 'You're in the second rondavel on the left,' he said jerkily, and turning abruptly, walked away from her.

Beth watched him go, shattered by the wave of self-pity that his words and his actions had aroused in her. How ironic that the Marchioness's hope of making him fall in love with her because she looked like Anne had been such a disastrous failure. Seeing a copy—albeit a

pale one—of the girl he believed he still loved had finally
shown him that this love was dead. Because she herself
loved Yorke, she was glad to hear he was now free of the
past, even though it meant the end of the faint hope she
had cherished. 'More fool me,' she thought wryly, and
walked up the path to her rondavel.

CHAPTER SIX

AFTER a few days in bed, the Marchioness was allowed to get up. She had accepted her enforced rest with surprising docility, due, Beth believed, to the fact that Yorke spent all his free time with her.

When he was in the rondavel Beth kept to her bedroom, but she could hear the constant hum of conversation and had wondered if her employer was using the time to persuade her grandson to return home.

Even now, several days after he had told Beth that seeing her had finally shown him he no longer loved his ex-fiancée, she still felt a deep sense of hurt, and wondered bitterly whether his new-found emotional freedom would last or if he would commit himself to another woman. This instantly brought Rowena Vale to mind. Without doubt she wanted Yorke. It was apparent in the way she spoke to him, the way she looked at him and the vague resentment she showed towards Beth. Perhaps it was an awareness of this that made Beth feel a similar resentment, for there was no real reason for her to dislike the Welsh girl. Yet she could not warm to her, and sensed that beneath the vivid smile and vivacious manner there lurked a hard and determined streak that would assert itself once Yorke was finally hers. And that he would become so seemed in very little doubt as the days lengthened into a week and Rowena became a daily visitor to the rondavel.

On the first occasion she had come with Yorke and had been prettily deferential as the Marchioness rambled on about the beauty of Powys and why she wanted its heir to return there. But after a few more visits she asked detailed questions about the running of the estate, surprising Beth by her probing catechism and knowledge.

'That grandson of mine makes a habit of meeting the wrong women,' the Marchioness said one evening as she retired early to bed, tired from the long drive they had taken that day. 'I didn't like Anne, but I am even less enamoured of Rowena.'

Beth concentrated on tidying the dressing-table.

'Stop lifting up my brushes and come and talk to me,' came the command.

'Not if you're going to discuss Yorke. I don't want to get involved in his affairs.'

'Why not? Don't you like him?' The black gaze was bright with curiosity, but Beth forced herself to meet it without flinching.

'I think he's charming, but he should be left to live his own life.'

'Don't tell me you agree with what he's doing!'

'I understand why he wants to stay here.'

'He's still running away from Anne. That's why.'

'I don't think so.' Beth paused, then decided it would not be indiscreet to mention something of what he had told her a few days ago. 'He'd willingly return to England if he could do the same sort of research there. But it seems to be impossible.'

'Is that what he told you or is it something you feel?'

'He told me.'

'Then why does he want me to believe he doesn't care about Powys?'

'Because he doesn't care in the same way that you do. And because he can't see himself leaving Mandama either.'

'What sort of life can he make here?'

'The kind of life he wants.'

'Do you think it will be with Rowena?'

Beth turned away. 'I suggest you ask him that yourself.'

The Marchioness moved restlessly against the pillows. 'She's intelligent, of course, but there is a hard streak in her. I have the impression she loves the title more than the man who goes with it.'

'Then you should encourage the romance,' Beth said firmly, delighted that she could hide her desire to run away and cry. 'If you're right about Rowena and she does marry Yorke, she will do her best to make him return to Powys. After all, you can't get much fun from a title in the middle of Africa!'

The Marchioness chuckled. 'Not as much fun as you would get from it in the jungle of café society! You have a point there, child. I will tackle Yorke about Rowena and see what he says.'

'Do you think that's tactful?'

'I'm too old to worry about being tactful. One of the few benefits of old age is that one no longer worries about offending anyone.'

'I can't believe you ever worried about that!' Beth commented and, seeing the Marchioness smile and then yawn, used it as an excuse to insist she turn out the light and go to sleep.

'What will you do?' the old lady asked her. 'It's too early for you to go to bed.'

'I'll go for a stroll. It's a lovely night and I feel in need of some cool air. This air-conditioning gives me a headache.'

'You do look peaky,' came the reply. 'I've noticed it the last couple of days.'

Beth murmured something indistinguishable and turned out the light, anxious to leave the room before any more pointed questions could be asked.

In the sitting-room she hesitated, wondering whether to go for a stroll—as she had said—or go to bed. Yet she had never felt more wakeful, with that curious restless energy that came from unhappiness. No wonder she looked peaky! It seemed ages since she had had a good night's sleep. Slipping her cardigan round her shoulders —more as a protection against the insects than the night air—she went out of the rondavel and wandered along the border of the camp.

On the other side of the wooden fence wild animals prowled, though, glimpsing the dark stretches of land through the bars of the slats, it all looked so peaceful that Beth could not believe it held any danger. Around her the daytime bustle of the camp had given way to the quietness of night, and a faint sound of music could be heard coming from the small hut used as a cinema, where incredibly ancient films were shown most nights and always attracted a large audience. It was not too late for her to slip in and pass away an hour, but as she moved across the gravel path to do so, she stopped. Once the show was ended someone would inevitably invite her back to their apartment or rondavel for a drink, and she could not face the prospect of making conversation when she was in such a depressed mood.

The determined friendliness of everyone at the Research Centre was something to which she was still not accustomed, and she marvelled at the lack of tension that existed and which she had not expected to find in such a close unit. But this might be due to the fact that people were here not through force of circumstance but because they wanted to be here. They all had the same sense of dedication and worked towards the same goal, from the lowliest technician to the Director himself. She thought of Dr Stallard, whom she had met for the first time last night. A tall, round-shouldered South African, he had been verbose in telling the Marchioness how much he appreciated having Yorke work with him, a piece of information that had in no way made the woman more amenable to his remaining here. Beth sighed. Perhaps the Marchioness was right to consider encouraging Rowena. The vital-looking Welsh girl could well succeed where everything else had failed. Rowena, Marchioness of Powys. Beth could visualise the dark-haired girl walking purposefully through the beautiful rooms or gliding across the lawns with children at her side. And what of Yorke? Would he be happy to manage the day-to-day affairs of the estate while he tried to hide his frustration at not being able to carry on with his research, or would his love for Rowena be strong enough to overcome all discontent?

A step sounded behind her and she swung round and saw the man of whom she had been thinking. She shrank back into the shadows, but it was too late, for he had seen her and was moving in her direction.

'So there you are,' he said as if he had been looking for her. 'My grandmother said you'd gone for a stroll.'

'Don't tell me you woke her up?'

'I'm afraid I did. I hadn't realised she would retire so early.'

'You shouldn't have come over so late,' Beth accused.

'I wasn't playing,' he said mildly. 'I was working.'

'You always are.'

'You sound unusually grumpy,' he commented. 'But you've been that way with me for days.'

She was surprised he had noticed her change of attitude and bitterly amused herself by trying to guess what he would say if he knew the cause of it. How desperately she longed to stand close to him and have his arms come round her. Only by holding herself aloof could she hope not to give herself away.

'Is it Mandama you don't like or is it something *I* have done?' he persisted.

'Neither. And I can't see why it should bother you either way. Companions are expected to be self-effacing creatures who——'

'You're talking rubbish and you know it!' He was unusually acerbic. 'Why do you talk about yourself in such a deprecating way? You're a young and desirable woman—not a middle-aged dowd!'

She felt an uplift of spirits but forced herself to see his compliment as a mere polite one. 'It's kind of you to say so,' she murmured.

'Kind of you to say so,' he mimicked. 'Is that the best you can do?'

'What do you want me to do?'

'I don't know! Just show some emotion, perhaps!'

With a movement which took her by surprise, he pulled her into his arms. She felt the warmth of his body and the throbbing of his heart—loud and heavy—through the thin silk of his shirt and the thinner silk of her dress. Then his mouth came down upon hers and his fingers bit deep into her shoulders. The kiss was so unexpected that she had no chance to feel surprise, and before she could attempt to draw away she was overwhelmed by a passion she had never before experienced. It carried her up on a tide of emotion that made her forget everything except this moment and the man with whom she was sharing it. Never had she been kissed with such intensity and she trembled and clung to him, unable to believe this was the Yorke she knew. Until now he had always been whimsical and mild, an occasional display of irritability the only sign he had given of emotion. She had known from the beginning that he was capable of feeling deeply, for only a man of intense passion could have gone on loving a woman who had left him years ago, but she had never associated him with the raw desire he was showing now, nor have believed that she herself would be capable of arousing it in him. Yet arouse it she did. It was evident in the burning pressure of his mouth, in the trembling of his body and the sudden way he rained kisses over her face, murmuring endearments which made no sense until he finally held her away from him and stared into her moonlight-drenched eyes.

'Beth?' he said huskily, the comment a question and not just the utterance of her name, as if he wanted reassurance from her that she would still speak to him. 'Forgive me. I didn't mean to frighten you.'

Only then did she realise she was shaking as though with fever, and knew he assumed it to be anger and not a sign of her need for him.

'I'm not angry,' she whispered.

'I'm glad. I wouldn't hurt you for the world.' His hand touched her cheek and his fingers ran gently along its smooth surface and down the side of her neck to rest in the hollow of her throat. 'You're such a gentle person, Beth. I would never want to frighten you. I won't do it again, I promise.'

Beth closed her eyes to hide the pain in them, marvelling that he had not recognised her response for what it was. 'Don't worry about it, Yorke.' Her voice was cool. 'You haven't scared me and I'm not angry with you because you kissed me. It didn't rate that much importance in my life.'

He looked at her with a puzzlement he made no attempt to disguise. 'I never know where I am with you. When I expect you to be gentle you round on me like a viper.'

'Perhaps you don't know me as well as you think.'

'I'm beginning to believe you're right. Maybe your gentle exterior is *only* an exterior; maybe you are quite different inside.'

'Why should it surprise you if I was? After all, I'd only be following the usual pattern of the women you know!' She heard his quick intake of breath and knew she had gone as far as she dared.

'You know nothing of the women I know.' For a long moment he stared down at her, looming so tall and dark that she was frightened by his strength. 'Nothing,' he repeated, and pushing her away from him, strode out of sight.

Slowly Beth returned to the rondavel. It was not only Yorke's kiss that had surprised her but the way he had apologised for it, and his angry reaction to her own attempt to make him believe that his kisses had meant nothing to her. That had obviously been the wrong thing to do. She frowned at this. Was Yorke the sort of man who believed every girl fell in love with him? He had never given her the impression of being conceited, yet there seemed no other reason for his anger.

She reached the whitewashed walls of her rondavel and quietly let herself in. She tiptoed across to her bedroom and was by the door when the Marchioness called her. Beth turned and went into the woman's room without putting on the light.

'Did you see Yorke, child? He came here looking for you.'

'Yes, I saw him.'

The bed creaked. 'What did he want?'

'Nothing. We just chatted.'

'Yorke never just chats. He hates small talk.'

Beth remained silent.

'We have been invited to a dinner party,' the Marchioness said suddenly. 'Did he tell you about it?'

'No.'

'Then you couldn't have done much chatting!'

'Perhaps he knew you would be telling me.' Beth moved over to the bed but kept away from the moonlight shining in through the window, anxious to keep her face in shadow. 'Who's giving the dinner party?'

'Dr Stallard, head of the Institute. It's in my honour.'

'Then you'd better get your beauty sleep.' Beth touched the bony hand lying on the coverlet. 'If you want me for anything during the night, call me. I'm a light sleeper.'

'And a restless one too. I've heard you tossing around in your bed.' There was a pause. 'You aren't fretting about anything, are you?'

'I have nothing to fret about,' Beth assured her, and went out quickly, murmuring goodnight from the doorway.

In her own room she stood by the window for a long time, staring out through the darkness at the other rondavels around them. How much longer would they be staying here, and if it were for more than a few weeks, would she be able to bear it? The thought of seeing Yorke day after day was intolerable, yet short of telling the Marchioness she wanted to leave her, she had no choice. Disconsolately she undressed and climbed into bed. Even when they returned to England, Yorke would still be constantly in her mind, for living at Powys would make it impossible to forget him. That meant she would have to find another job and, more important still, have to find a good excuse for leaving this one. How hurt the Marchioness would be when she heard. Yet it was impossible to tell her the real reason for fear she told Yorke. The thought made Beth writhe with shame. How could she have allowed herself to be swept off her feet like a romantic sixteen-year-old? If only she was as prosaic as she looked. As she thought this, she remembered that less than an hour ago Yorke had called her a lovely and desirable young woman. It was a compliment she longed to believe, yet felt unable to accept. As if she, Beth Miller, could ever be called desirable! Tears poured down her cheeks, but she did not wipe them away, knowing that more would follow.

'Yorke,' she whispered silently. 'I've got to forget you, but I don't know how I can.'

CHAPTER SEVEN

As befitted his position, Dr Stallard occupied the only house in the Mandama Research Centre. It was a wooden, two-storied one and was furnished with his own furniture. He was a widower, but well catered for by two African servants and invitations to his dinner parties were much sought after by everyone at the Centre.

Since Beth could not avoid seeing Yorke again, she was glad she could do so in a room full of people, and the determination to show how meaningless he was to her decided her to wear the red dress. What did she care if it reminded him of the girl he had once loved? Let him suffer, the way he was making her suffer. Yet he was unaware of the havoc he had caused in her life, and admitting this she decided to take off the red dress. She was halfway to the wardrobe when the bedroom door opened and the Marchioness came in.

'I'm glad you are wearing that again,' she said. 'It suits you.'

'Because it makes me look like Yorke's ex-fiancée?'

A flush stained the bony cheeks, but the older woman met Beth's gaze forthrightly. 'Who told you?'

'Rowena.'

'She hasn't seen you in that dress.'

Beth shrugged. 'She told me I look like Anne and Yorke has already told me that red was her favourite colour. It didn't require much intelligence to put two and two together.'

'Are you angry with me?'

'Did you expect me not to be? Maybe all the dresses you bought me will make me look like a carbon copy of another woman?'

'Don't talk like that. I admit I was deliberate when I bought you the red dress, but none of the others are anything like the ones Anne would have worn.'

'You mean you have allowed me to have a personality of my own?'

'My dear child!' The cane in the Marchioness's hand was trembling. 'I didn't do it to hurt you. I never thought you would find out.'

'Did you think I'd never find out I looked like Anne?'

'You are a similar type,' the Marchioness said slowly, 'but you don't really look like her. Not when one knows you.'

'Who'd bother to know *me*?' Beth said, still hurt.

The dark eyes narrowed. 'So much emotion over a dress? Are you sure you aren't upset about something else?'

Beth turned her head, afraid she had given herself away. 'I don't like being made a fool,' she murmured.

'I am deeply sorry.'

There was a tremor in the thin voice that made Beth regret she had lost her temper. It was wrong to blame the Marchioness for doing all she could to make her grandson realise the existence of other women. Beth's hands clenched at her sides. Would she have been used as bait if the existence of Rowena had been known?

'We mustn't be late for the party,' she said quickly, and put out her arm as support.

Dr Stallard's living room was already crowded when they arrived, and their entry resembled that of the Israelites crossing the Red Sea, for the waves of people parted to let the Marchioness flow majestically between them. Their host was younger than Beth had remembered from her first meeting with him; though as tall as Yorke, he did not give that impression because of the slight stoop to his shoulders, which also gave him a more gentle air than the younger man. But the gentleness did not extend to his eyes which were a pale blue and could best have been described as frosty, though they were now regarding Beth with noticeable warmth.

'Charming,' he murmured, his hand lingering on hers a moment longer than was necessary. 'A most delightful dress, Miss Miller.'

'I wouldn't dare wear it if you had any bulls in the Kruger Park!'

'We have,' he smiled, 'but *inside* the compound!'

She laughed and he echoed it. 'You'll forgive me if I do not spend much time with you this evening?' he continued. 'Being a host without a hostess means I have to do double duty.'

'Please don't apologise,' she said quickly. 'I don't expect you to entertain me.'

'There's nothing I would like better.' He beckoned a servant. 'What will you have to drink, Miss Miller?'

'Something long—but alcoholic,' bravura made her add.

'Then I suggest a Tom Collins.' He waited until she had taken her first sip, and then with a regretful smile moved away to talk to some new arrivals. Left alone, Beth moved closer to the wall. Conversation wafted around her and snatches of it were loud enough for her to hear.

'You know darn well that research eats up the money, and if Stallard can't raise it . . .'

'You'd think the Government . . .'

'Publicity is the only answer, lots of publicity. That's why ...'

Beth's thoughts turned inwards inevitably to Yorke, whom she glimpsed through a gap in the crowd, talking to the Marchioness and Rowena. Tonight the Welsh girl looked dramatic in a flowing purple kaftan that made the best of her dark looks and emphasised her strong character, which was as much a part of her attraction as her tall, well formed body. Personality was as much a part of beauty as beauty itself, Beth thought dejectedly, and wished she had worn something other than the bright red dress. A grey shroud would have been more appropriate to her mood and personality. Some people were born to shine, some to glimmer and others to give no light at all, and to fight against this was to emulate King Canute. She half smiled at the thought and, glancing up again, met Yorke's eyes. Even at a distance they had the power to shake her like an electric current and she quickly averted her head and stepped forward to join the conversation of two young technicians standing nearby. They were delighted to explain to her the intricacies of their work and she listened with pretended enthusiasm, still keeping beside them when dinner was announced and they moved into the dining room.

The room was too small to have accommodated everyone at one large table, so half a dozen smaller ones had been arranged round the room and on the verandah itself. The early dusk of the tropics had descended and candles glittered on white clothes, giving the scene a romantic air that Beth found pleasing, though disturbing to her mood. There were place cards at the tables and she saw she was sitting between the two men with whom she had already been talking. The Marchioness, Yorke and Rowena were sitting at Dr Stallard's table and she was thankful Yorke had his back to her, though the sight of his broad shoulders and silky black head filled her with the same excitement as if she had been staring into his lean dark face. She forced herself not to look in his direction, but like a rabbit trained upon the eye of a snake, she could not help continually glancing that way, and invariably met Dr Stallard's eyes each time.

The meal itself was nothing exceptional; the beef, though tender, was tasteless, and the vegetables were cooked in too much water, which again was a fault she had encountered frequently out here. But there was ample wine and it flowed freely, loosening tongues and making the conversation more boisterous. Coffee was served at the tables, but immediately afterwards they readjourned to the living room, where she was steered towards a settee by the younger of the two technicians.

'I can't let you go on monopolising Miss Miller.' Dr Stallard barred their way. His face was flushed and it made him look younger than the fifty she knew him to be. Even his eyes seemed more blue as they twinkled at her.

'If you're pulling rank on me, sir, I'll have to give in gracefully,' the young man said with a laugh.

'There must be *some* compensations in the seniority of age!' With a hand on her arm, Dr Stallard led Beth to a corner of the room by an open window.

'I'm glad you rescued me,' she smiled. 'I was beginning to become an expert on staphylo—something or other.'

'Ted is still young enough to be an enthusiast, but he should learn not to bore pretty women with his own pet obsessions.'

'Aren't you an enthusiast too? I thought everyone who worked here was.'

'Age has tempered my enthusiasm.'

'Why bring age into it?' she smiled. 'I prefer the words "reason" and "experience".'

'So do I,' he agreed, 'but looking at you I feel every one of my years and regret ten of them!'

There was an intenseness in his look that made her blush, and the light answer she had been about to give died on her lips.

'How are you enjoying your stay at Mandama?' He bridged the silence with small talk and she told him politely she was enjoying it very much, though she wished she knew more of what was being done.

'We don't cater for visitors,' he explained. 'Our work tends to lack visual excitement and our experiments are generally long and tedious ones. If we *could* generate more excitement here, we would find it much easier to raise money.'

'I didn't know you were short of money.'

'One never has enough money for research. I have just returned from a tour of the States where I went to try and raise some.'

'Did you have any luck?'

'I'm still waiting to hear. I haven't——' He broke off as his houseboy came towards and whispered in his ear. 'Fate must have overheard me talking to you,' he said, looking at Beth. 'There's a call come in from the States now. Please excuse me while I take it.' Lightly his hand touched her arm. 'Please stay where you are. I'll be right back.'

He went away and Beth turned to gaze through the window. She had enjoyed talking to John Stallard, as she always enjoyed talking to people older than herself. It came from being the only child of elderly parents, she knew, as well as the fact that, from the time her mother had become ill, she had helped her father take care of his elderly parishioners.

'What are you thinking, Beth?'

She knew without looking round that Yorke had come to stand beside her, and it required all her will power not to move away from him. Instead she turned to face him, as if he were just another man in the room and not the one for whom she desperately ached. 'People always want to know my thoughts,' she replied.

'Because you look so charming when you think.'

'I had my back to you!'

'The back was charming too! Tell me, what was preoccupying you so deeply?'

'I was thinking of myself as a child and how serious and dull I must have been.'

'Serious and sweet,' Yorke corrected.

'Dull,' she repeated. 'The way I am now.'

'You must be fishing for compliments!'

'Don't tell me you're still letting my clothes fool you? Beneath this disguise, I'm——'

'No,' he interrupted. 'I'm not fooled by the clothes. Maybe I was, the first few times I saw you, but very soon I saw your own personality come shining through.'

'Shining!' she said with a dry laugh. 'That's the wrong word for a start.'

'You enjoy being self-deprecating, don't you?'

'I was being realistic.'

'Is that why you wore the red dress again?'

Her cheeks flamed. It was hopeless to pretend she did not know what he meant, and instead she grasped the nettle firmly. 'I put it on to annoy you.'

His eyes glittered. 'I rather assumed you had.'

'Well, now you know for sure.'

'Why do you want to hurt me?'

'Perhaps hurt is the wrong word. Perhaps I was just

testing you.' He said nothing and she knew he was waiting for her to continue. 'You said my being here had made you realise the past was dead. I—I wasn't sure if you were being truthful, so I——'

'Decided to test me, by wearing that dress? Does that mean you're interested in finding out the result?'

'My interest is one of curiosity,' she said lightly.

'Only curiosity?'

Before she could reply John Stallard was beside them, beaming widely. 'That was a call from the States. Apparently the speech I gave in Houston was a bigger success than I realised.' He glanced at Beth. 'It was to a convention of millionaires, if you can believe such a thing! I was trying to persuade them that putting their money into medical research in South Africa was as worthy as promoting the arts.'

'You mean you've raised the money you want?'

'Not quite that,' he said, 'but four Texans are arriving here the day after tomorrow, and there's a good chance of them giving us an endowment.'

'That's excellent news, John.' Yorke's delight equalled that of his Director. 'They'll be staying here, of course?'

'Of course. I will have to rearrange my schedule so that I can spend as much time with them as possible. You too, Yorke. As my next in command and with a title...'

'I knew you'd want to use my title,' Yorke said dryly.

'Naturally. Americans love anything that smacks of heritage.'

Yorke shrugged. 'Tell me the worst. Who exactly are they?'

'Two of them are bachelor brothers, name of Pollock. They own a uranium mine.'

'And the other two?'

'A husband and wife. He's a beef baron called Coram.'

Beth was looking at Yorke as John Stallard spoke, and she saw the colour seep from his face, leaving only the tan of a skin with no blood behind it. Stallard was too busy seeing dollars pouring into Mandama to have eyes for anything else, and he went on talking about the Texans, unaware that Yorke was standing as if turned to stone.

'Coram's wife is English,' the Director went on, 'so you will at least have something in common. Charming girl too, and I'm pretty sure she has great influence over her husband.'

He paused as the Marchioness and Rowena joined them and Beth, watching Rowena look at Yorke, knew she was also aware that he had received a shock. But Stallard was speaking again: repeating his news to the Marchioness who, unlike her grandson, gave a loud exclamation.

'We are well acquainted with Anne Coram,' she said harshly. 'Had it not been for your offer to Yorke to come out here for two years, she and——'

'I don't think John needs to have a blow-by-blow account of my past,' Yorke cut in smoothly. He was in control of himself again, though he still looked grey-faced. 'Anne and I were once engaged,' he said lightly to the man beside him, 'so Coram might not like it if I'm too much on the scene.'

For the first time Beth saw John Stallard at a disadvantage, but he was quick to hide it. 'Let's play it by ear. That's the best way.'

'Isn't it all rather a storm in a teacup?' Rowena smiled, only the tossing of her head giving indication of temper held in check. 'I mean, it was more than five years since you were engaged to her, Yorke. And I don't see why Coram should be jealous. After all,' Rowena asked, 'he won her, didn't he?'

'Indeed he did,' the Marchioness's smile was faintly wolfish. 'How clever of you to pinpoint the situation with such logic.'

'Men are never logical when it comes to romance,' Rowena retorted. 'They romanticise far more than women.'

'You and Beth should get together,' Yorke said quietly. 'She thinks so too.'

Rowena favoured Beth with a disdainful stare, her hard brown eyes raking over the red dress and Beth's soft fair hair which she had pulled back into a bunch of curls at the nape of her neck, another abortive attempt to look sophisticated. 'Are you pandering to Yorke's illusions or trying to foster them for yourself?' the Welsh girl said so softly that only Beth could hear her.

'Neither,' Beth replied equally softly, and fixed her attention on the Marchioness. 'I don't want to break up the party, but it's rather late and I think we should leave.'

'There is no reason for *you* to go,' the Marchioness said, and unexpectedly put her hand on Rowena's arm. 'Come, my dear, you can escort me to my rondavel, and we can continue our little chat.'

With commendable grace Rowena hid her annoyance at being taken away from the group and she gave her arm to the Marchioness, who leaned on it heavily, to be led away with John Stallard bringing up the rear.

'You've made a hit with John,' Yorke remarked as he and Beth were left alone.

'Does that surprise you?'

'Not at all. You would appeal to most men.'

Her soft mouth hardened. 'Is that why I'm still single at twenty-four?'

'I think that's your own fault. Men are like bees, you know. They won't pause at a bud, no matter how beautiful a flower it's going to be. They go for those that are already opened.'

The comment unsettled her, but she managed not to show it. 'Is John a highly intelligent bee, then?'

Dark eyes narrowed as they slowly moved over her body, almost seeming to undress her. 'Let's say that the petals are unfolding.' He came a step closer. 'Beth, there's something I want——'

'Don't let's talk about me any more,' she interrupted breathlessly. 'I'm much more interested in knowing how you feel about seeing Mrs Coram again.'

For an instant Yorke stared into her face. 'You would have made an awful dentist,' he said on an indrawn breath. 'You'd go on trying to find a nerve in a dead tooth!'

It was such an apt simile that she had the grace to blush.

'Anyway,' he went on tightly, 'why are you so concerned about my feelings for Anne? Are you jealous of me?'

Her heart gave such a loud thump she was afraid he might hear it. 'I'm fond of your grandmother,' she said swiftly, 'and I don't want her to get upset.'

'Still the ideal companion!' he taunted. 'But you can set your mind at rest. As I've already told you—though it seems you still don't believe me—my feelings for Anne are dead.'

'Is that why you went as pale as a ghost when you learned she was coming here?'

'I was surprised. No more than that.' His lips curved

into an unpleasant sneer. 'You'll soon have the chance of seeing for yourself that I'm not lying.'

'I'd find it easier to believe you if you returned to Powys,' she said.

'My refusing to do that has nothing to do with Anne,' he grated. 'What more must I do to convince you?'

'I'm not the one who needs convincing,' she said wildly, 'it's your grandmother. Personally I don't care what you do. At least I care about Powys—not about you.'

'I'm glad to see there's something that can arouse you,' he said dryly. 'Even if it's only a house.'

With a half salute he moved away from her, and she remained by the wall, wishing that the trembling of her limbs would stop so that she would slip away and find somewhere quiet where she need not pretend to a calmness she did not feel.

'I'm glad I've managed to find you alone.' John Stallard was beside her once more, and with an effort she forced herself to smile at him, from the corner of her eyes seeing that Rowena had returned to the room and was standing close to Yorke. She was talking to him intently, and though it was not possible to guess what she was saying, there was no doubting the proprietorial gesture of the hand she placed on his arm.

Following her gaze, John Stallard looked at Yorke. 'The Coram visit will be even more interesting than I had envisaged. Rowena doesn't like competition and I rather think Yorke will be in for a pretty rough passage.'

'I should imagine he's a good navigator,' Beth said. 'He must be, to have stayed single all these years.'

'He is devoted to his work. It's only in the last year that he has given any sign of not finding it totally absorbing.' He rubbed the side of his chin. 'Yes, things should become quite interesting.'

'Do you always regard the people you work for as guinea-pigs?' Beth inquired, and was rewarded by John Stallard's startled look.

'I wasn't aware of it until you just raised the point,' he said slowly, 'but I take your point, Miss Miller.' He stooped towards her. 'Beth?' he said questioningly and, at her nod, straightened again. 'You must call me John,' he added. 'It's a long time since a woman has done that.'

CHAPTER EIGHT

BETH expected the Marchioness to comment on Anne Coram's arrival, and she was not surprised when, returning to the rondavel at midnight—escorted there by John Stallard and briefly but warmly kissed goodnight—she was summoned to the old lady's bedroom.

'I have been waiting up for you,' the Marchioness said.

'I offered to come back with you,' Beth pointed out.

'I didn't want to take you away from Yorke.'

'I was with Dr Stallard,' Beth said dryly.

'So I have just gathered! He is too old for you, child.'

'He isn't old,' Beth replied with a smile, 'nor is he for me.'

'He would like to be. I saw him making sheep's eyes at you!'

'Shall we talk about it in the morning?' Beth moved to the door, but was stopped by an imperious gesture.

'I am worried about Yorke,' the Marchioness said. 'It will be the first time he has seen Anne since she left him.'

Beth did not feel she could make any useful comment and waited to see what else was coming.

'Do you think he still loves her?'

'Don't you think that's a question he can answer much better than I can?'

'I don't believe him—whatever he says—and I don't trust my own judgment.'

'How can you trust mine?' Beth protested. 'I hardly know him.'

107

'You are intuitive and sensitive.' The bird-like eyes peered at her. 'Tell me, does he give the impression of a man who is in love?'

'Yes, he does.' Only as she heard her reply—which seemed to come out of its own accord—did Beth realise the truth of what she had said. Yorke did act like a man in love. He had the edginess and irritability of someone who was working his way through an emotional problem. And there were his odd moods too: one moment gay, the next angry with an anger that seemed to come from nothing. All this bespoke an emotional unrest. 'It's either Anne Coram or Rowena Vale,' she added.

'Well, Rowena would be better than Anne,' came the grudging reply, 'though she isn't the girl I'd have chosen for him.'

'I think your grandson is old enough to do his own choosing.'

'Who has been stopping him, then?' the Marchioness snapped. 'If only he would go ahead and choose! Even if he won't come back to Powys, at least if he marries and has children the family will continue.'

The words signified a change of attitude on the Marchioness's part, an acceptance that her grandson might well elect to live his life away from his ancestral home. But if she knew the line would continue and could believe that one day Yorke's sons might return to Powys, this would give her the peace of mind for which she was looking.

'I'm glad you are being realistic,' Beth said, and moved resolutely to the door. 'Now we have resolved that little problem, do you think you could go to sleep?'

'It won't be resolved until I have seen Yorke with Anne. That is the only way I will know how he really feels. He may be able to disguise his emotions and his behaviour, but he can't hide the look in his eyes.'

Beth closed the door, wishing she could as easily close out the thoughts that were going to torment her in the days ahead.

It was not only the Marchioness who was anxious to know Yorke's reactions to Anne Coram. She too would be watching for them, eager to see if there was any truth in his assertion that he no longer loved the girl. Yet even if he didn't, it meant nothing in her life. All it would mean was a bright future for Rowena.

For the next two days Beth went out of her way to avoid being alone with Yorke, a task made easier by John Stallard's eagerness to spend all his free time with her. On the third day he offered to take her and the Marchioness on a drive through the Park, an offer which the Marchioness refused, pleading fatigue, but insisted that Beth accept. Since anything was better than the prospect of seeing Yorke, Beth did not demur, and making sure the Marchioness would not be left alone, she set out with John before any of the personnel at Mandama were astir.

The weather was perfect. A cool breeze drew off the worst of the heat and the animals behaved as though they had received instructions. Herds of elephants abounded—some knocking down tree trunks in front of her delighted eyes and some ambling around a waterhole. Tall, elegant giraffes loped across the grass on incredibly thin long legs, pursued by what seemed to be several hundred zebras: a moving river of black and white. There were crocodiles too, basking on the banks of the Sabie River and floating like harmless logs in the dark water, occasionally lifting a jaw to show they were not wood but a living trap waiting for bait. But it was two lions who gave her the most memorable moments. They lay on the side of the road, like two huge and lazy cats, and John Stallard was able to draw up almost abreast of them.

Beth watched in amusement as the lion moved closer to his mate and began to lick her coat. The lioness accepted his caress without returning it, and then signified her boredom by turning over on her side and resting her golden head on her paws.

'She's telling him she doesn't want him at the moment,' John murmured.

'He doesn't seem to be taking the hint,' Beth chuckled as the lion edged himself closer to his mate and resumed licking her.

'It still won't have any effect,' John said. 'Like most females, this one is going to make him wait before she succumbs!'

'Unlike me,' Beth thought, knowing that if Yorke had wanted to make love to her, she would never have had the strength of mind to pretend she did not want him. But it was madness to relate everything in terms of Yorke and herself. Surely she would be able to put him out of her mind once she was no longer near him? She must have made some exclamation, for John assumed it to be impatience and went to start the car.

'No,' she protested, 'let's watch them a little longer.'

'You like lions?'

'I adore them. They're so calm and strong.'

'Thank heavens you didn't say cuddly! I had visions of restraining you from getting out of the car and wrapping your arms round them.'

'The thought did cross my mind,' she teased. 'What would happen if I did?'

'They'd tear you apart. They aren't big pussy cats, my dear. They're wild and ferocious animals.'

'Yet they don't mind the cars and they ignore the people watching them.'

'They're used to cars, and as long as people remain inside them, *they'll* be ignored too. But if anyone stepped out ...' He shuddered. 'I sometimes get nightmares at the thought.' He set the car in motion again and this time she did not stop him, though she looked back through the rear window to watch the two lions until they were out of sight.

They stopped for lunch at one of the other camps and rested for a while in the shaded patio of a fever tree. But John was anxious to show her as much of the Park as possible, and while most of the visitors were still resting, they resumed their journey, this time in an air-conditioned car.

'If you really want to see big game you should go to Kenya,' he informed her.

'I go where I'm taken,' she said. 'I'm extremely lucky to be here and not in some chilly British seaside resort!'

'I'm the lucky one. If you hadn't come to Mandama I would never have met you.' His smile was tender and he took one hand from the wheel and placed it over hers.

She forced herself not to draw back, though she was determined not to give him any encouragement. But he did not need encouragement, for he had sufficient of his own.

'You know I'm falling in love with you, Beth?'

'But you've only just met me,' she protested.

'Falling in love doesn't take long.' He paused. 'I suppose you find it surprising because I'm old?'

'You aren't old,' she said, unwilling to let him hurt himself. 'It's just that I don't know what you can see in me.'

'Don't you ever look in your mirror?'

'Too often to fool myself that I'm anything special.'

'Then you must be blind—or else your eyes are misted by visions of busty blondes.' He squeezed her fingers. 'I'll be delighted to enumerate your qualities.'

'You wouldn't convince me.'

He slowed down the car and stopped. 'Would this convince you?' he asked, and drew her gently into his arms, kissing her in a way that was not gentle at all. For a moment she struggled against him and then went passive, surprised by the strength of his hold and his ardour. How deceiving appearances were, she thought involuntarily, and knew a momentary fear which died the instant he released her.

'Sorry about that,' he said jerkily. 'It seems I'm not as old as I believed.' He leaned an elbow on the wheel. 'What are my chances with you, Beth?'

'I don't know,' she lied. 'I—I haven't thought of you in that way.'

'But you don't dislike me?'

'Of course not. But I don't love you,' she added candidly, 'and it would be wrong of me to give you any hope.'

'Do you love anyone else?'

She wondered whether to go on lying and then decided to tell him part of the truth. 'Yes, I do,' she whispered, 'but he isn't in love with me. He—he doesn't even know how I feel about him.'

'And are you prepared to live the rest of your life with an unrequited love?'

'I don't know. I haven't—I can't think that far ahead.'

'He must be blind—whoever he is—and very stupid not to know what he's missing.'

'I'm easy to overlook,' she said, smiling slightly.

'So are diamonds in the ground. But when they are cut

and polished no one can ignore them.'

'That's a rather back-handed compliment,' she said, seeing the humour of his remark and using it to lessen the emotion between them. 'Are you suggesting I'd improve with cutting and polishing?'

'The cut and thrust of love would make you sparkle! I meant no more than that.'

'It was a nice compliment anyway. I'll treasure it.'

'You make it sound as if you've already put me into your past.' He caught her hand again. 'But I want to be in your future. Don't dismiss what I've said to you, Beth.'

'I'm not, but——'

'Does it have anything to do with the fact that I live at Mandama?'

'Of course not. If I loved a man I'd live with him anywhere.'

'You mean that too,' he said softly, and went to take hold of her again. But her involuntary movement away from him made him change his mind, and he switched on the ignition and drove for several miles in silence. There were many things Beth could have said to him, but she did not know how to phrase them, and it was on their return journey—with the buildings of Mandama visible on the horizon—that she tried to make him see it would be unwise for him to go on thinking of her.

'You can't stop me from hoping,' he said. 'And until the day I hear you've married someone else, I will go on doing it.'

Tears filled her eyes and she blinked them away. 'I wish you wouldn't. You make me feel guilty.'

'You should be happy, not guilty. You've made me realise I'm still a virile man!' She smiled through her tears and he touched her cheek. 'That's better. I don't like to see you cry.' The gates of the Research Centre swung open and they drove through and into the compound.

'Will you and the Marchioness dine with me tonight?' he asked, retaining her hand as he helped her from the car. 'I will see if Yorke and Rowena can come along too.'

It was on Beth's lips to refuse, but she forced back the words. John was no fool, and having told him she was in love with someone, he might easily put two and two together and reach the right conclusion. 'That will be fine,' she said lightly. 'I'm sure the Marchioness will be delighted.'

'And you? Will you be delighted too?'

She saw he had taken no notice of her earlier warning to forget her, and knew that for the rest of her stay at Mandama he would try and make her fall in love with him. It was a knowledge that added to the weight of the depression she was already carrying around with her. She loved Yorke but he loved someone else, and John Stallard loved her, not knowing that she ... Ruefully, she admitted that it had the makings of another *Midsummer Night's Dream*, with Rowena playing the mischievous Puck. Or was that the Marchioness's role?

'I'll be delighted to have dinner with you,' she sighed, and felt guilty as she saw the gratified smile on his face.

The dinner party was less difficult than she had envisaged, for both John and Yorke went out of their way to explain the workings of Mandama and the research that was being carried out there. Even Rowena had something to contribute, and it was easy to see that she was an exceptionally capable biologist with a distinct flair for spotting the unusual and then following it up with tenacity. It was the same tenacity, Beth saw, with which she was pursuing Yorke, and she wondered whether the older girl would be as successful in this as she was with everything else she did.

Certainly Yorke gave the impression tonight that he found Rowena an exciting companion, for he was noticeably attentive to her and answered all her questions about his childhood at Powys. It was obvious he had not done so before, for Rowena listened to him avidly, and watching the Marchioness's face, Beth knew that the old lady was reconciling herself to accepting the Welsh girl as her future granddaughter. Not the ideal one, perhaps, but better than having Yorke remain a bachelor and the family die out. Beth set down her fork, unable to swallow any of the ice cream on her plate, and John looked at her with concern.

'Don't you like it?'

'It's excellent,' she smiled, 'but I'm full.'

'Your cook has excelled herself,' Rowena commented.

'I told her I was having some very special people to dinner,' he replied, looking at Beth as he spoke.

It was a look which everyone at the table saw and all interpreted in the same way, and Beth was aware of Yorke regarding her sourly, though why he should feel that way was beyond her. Was it because he knew she had no genuine feelings for John? If that were the case then he had no right to be condemnatory, for he was behaving equally falsely with Rowena: one moment he insisted he had no thought in mind except work, and the next moment he went out of his way to give the girl the opposite impression. Quite obviously he was putting on an act in preparation for Anne Coram's arrival.

Beth glanced at Rowena, wondering if she too was aware of this. After all, what better way was there of making an ex-fiancée believe she was no longer loved than by presenting her with the woman who had replaced her in his affections? Yet for Yorke to play such a game was courting danger. He might be putting on an act, but Rowena wasn't doing so. She was playing for keeps, not for pretence, and if Yorke did not realise this, for himself, he must be very insensitive indeed.

'By this time tomorrow our Texan visitors should be here,' John said as they moved into the sitting-room for coffee. 'I've mapped out an itinerary of the things I would like them to see.' He crossed over to his desk and came back with a sheet of paper which he handed to Yorke. 'Do you have any suggestions to add to it?'

Dark eyes glanced at it. 'It seems pretty comprehensive to me. I see you've marked them in for a week. Do you think they will stay that long?'

'It's impossible to say.'

'What are you actually hoping to get out of them?' Rowena asked, her bright face alight with curiosity. She looked particularly striking tonight, in a wide-skirted purple dress with full bell sleeves.

'I'd like to build a new laboratory and extend our accommodation for workers. We're very under-staffed here, and if I can offer better married quarters, I'm sure I can get the people I want.'

'Your Texans might not want to put up money for staff quarters,' Yorke drawled. He was lounging back in an easy chair. Behind him a standard lamp shed its light on his hair, making it glisten like a jet but throwing long shadows down his face that gave him a Machiavellian expression. 'Millionaires have a habit of wanting to designate how their money is used, and they might well prefer to endow Mandama with a swimming pool or an air-conditioned movie house!'

'It will be our job to convince them otherwise,' John

replied, and seated himself next to Beth, looking so much at home beside her that Rowena flung Yorke a quizzical look and he in turn stared broodingly at his Director. Almost as if she resented his withdrawn air, Rowena walked over and perched herself on the arm of his chair.

'I would like you to come and have a look at Inge,' she murmured.

'What's wrong with her?' Yorke asked instantly.

'She's developed a temperature after the heart transplant. I'm a bit worried about her.'

He stood up immediately and looked directly at Beth, almost as if he knew her unspoken question. 'Inge's a monkey. But she won't die—except from natural causes —so you needn't look so stricken.'

'I—I can't help it,' Beth stammered. 'I hate the idea of animals being used for experiments.'

'Would you rather that children died of——' Yorke stopped. 'It's a point that one can argue on indefinitely.'

'Not tonight,' Rowena said sweetly. 'We have other things to do.'

'Will you be gone long?' the Marchioness asked.

'Possibly,' said Yorke. 'I won't want to leave the monkey alone.'

'I'll see the Marchioness doesn't have too late a night,' John Stallard intervened.

'Thanks.' Yorke spoke to his Director but looked at Beth sardonically, an expression which she refused to acknowledge. How dared he act as if he were a leper! Or was he annoyed because he saw her as his grandmother's keeper and felt she was failing in her duties?

Swiftly she rose. 'I think we might as well leave too,' she said, and put her hand on John Stallard's arm as he stood up beside her.

'Such an early end to the evening,' he protested.

'It's been a long day for me,' she murmured, 'but a lovely one.'

'I hope there will be many more.'

Conscious of Yorke still in the room, she gave the older man a brilliant smile. 'So do I, John. So do I.'

CHAPTER NINE

THE three Texan millionaires arrived in a chauffeur-driven Cadillac, followed by a second car bearing their luggage and a sallow-faced woman who turned out to be Anne Coram's maid. Beth did not see them arrive, for the Marchioness had decided to spend the day in bed in preparation for the dinner party which John Stallard was giving again that evening, but the entire Research Station was agog with it, from the amount of monogrammed luggage to the crates of special whisky and tinned food brought as a present for the medical staff at Mandama.

Yorke called to collect his grandmother at eight o'clock and Beth was still in her room changing. She had chosen to wear the simplest dress she had with her and used the minimum of make-up, determined that tonight she was going to be as much like her old self as possible and not the way the Marchioness wanted her to look. Yet strangely she could not revert to the quiet self-effacing creature she had been a few months ago. It was as if her daily contact with her employer's abrasive personality had sharpened her own. Even her hair, long, soft and mouse-coloured, was now obstinately going its own way. The ends curled upwards and were tipped with silver where they had been bleached by the sun. Her skin too was sun-kissed and looked golden by contrast with her coffee silk dress.

She opened the door and went into the next room. Yorke looked round as he heard her step, his eyes half closing as he surveyed her slim fairness. She was breathing quickly and her breasts rose and fell, their movement discernible beneath the soft material of her dress.

'I'm sorry to have kept you waiting,' she said breathlessly.

He shrugged, then swung back to look at his grandmother, resplendent in black. 'Anne knows you're here.'

'You've seen her?' The question was sharp.

'I thought it best to get the introductions over as quickly as possible,' he said casually. 'I went round to Coram's quarters as soon as they had settled in.'

'I don't suppose she was surprised to see you?'

'You suppose right.' Eyelids masked Yorke's eyes, making their glitter barely discernible. 'She admitted that she knew I was here. Anne was always truthful, if nothing else.'

'Her only saving grace,' said the Marchioness. 'Is that why she has come here—to get you back?'

Beth made a movement towards her bedroom. If Yorke and his grandmother were going to talk about Anne Coram, she had no wish to listen.

'Don't go,' he said abruptly, 'the conversation is finished.' He switched off the lights and then opened the front door.

The walk to John Stallard's house was completed in silence and Beth was conscious only of the fast beating of her heart and the wish to run away. Yet in the end curiosity overcame her nervousness and, entering the sitting-room and seeing Anne Coram, she felt all her fears justified. But with the fear came amazement at seeing someone who could well have passed for her sister. A slightly older sister, it was true, she decided cattily, but also—and here her honesty got the better of her—an infinitely more beautiful one. She had the same slender figure and fair colouring, but had used every artifice from her limitless bank balance to increase her allure and, from the tips of her arched feet with their slender ankles, to the top of her shining fair hair—artfully silvered—she was an exquisite and vital work of art, as vivid in her own blonde way as Rowena was in her dark one. No two women were more opposite in their appearance and none could have had a greater mutual dislike of each other. Beth sensed it as soon as she walked into the room, and so did Yorke, for she felt him grow tense, though his voice—when he made the introductions— held its normal drawling tones.

'Grandmother you already know, Anne, but I'd like you to meet Beth Miller, a friend of the family.'

Anne slightly raised delicate eyebrows, a gesture that made it obvious she had already ascertained Beth's position.

'Of course I remember the Marchioness,' she said huskily, and bent forward to kiss the wrinkled cheek. 'You don't look any different from the way you did on the first day I met you.'

'*You* do,' came the forthright reply. 'Though I see that red is still your favourite colour.'

'You remember?'

'Everything.'

Anne Coram gave a tinkling laugh that managed not to sound amused. 'Your sense of humour is still the same, I see.'

'I've heard a great deal about English humour,' a deep voice said, and Beth found that a short, chunky man had come to stand beside them. From the way he regarded Anne Coram she knew at once that he was her husband, and was surprised to find him so different from the way she had imagined him. He was older than she had expected—nearer fifty than forty—with close-cropped grey hair and muscular shoulders that not even a well-cut dinner jacket could hide. His face was heavy-jowled but his mouth was nicely shaped and sensitive, and his warm brown eyes surveyed you with open candour which, she felt sure, was one of his particular traits. He bowed deferentially towards the Marchioness but gripped Beth's hand in a bone-grating grasp which made her wince.

Seeing it, Anne gave a low-throated laugh. 'One day someone is going to sue Jack for broken bones!'

'As long as it isn't my wife, I'll be able to afford it,' her husband quipped. 'You're the only one who can make a pauper of me!'

'It doesn't seem to deter men from marrying,' the Marchioness commented.

'It does some,' Jack Coram grinned. 'Or else they get their lawyers to draw up special documents ahead of time which both parties have to sign. Then if the marriage goes wrong, all the legal hassle is over. Wife takes the amount of money originally agreed, and husband goes in search of another one to take her place.'

'How cold-blooded you make it sound!' Beth burst out.

'I agree with you.' Shrewd eyes surveyed her. 'That's why I ignored my lawyers' advice when I married Anne. If she wants to do so, she could take the pants off me!'

'You're a trusting man,' Yorke drawled. He was still standing closer to Beth than to anyone else and gave the impression that it was deliberate.

'That's what all my friends said before they met Anne,' the Texan drawled back. 'But now they envy me.'

'What Jack has omitted to mention,' Anne said, 'is that most of his wealth is tied up in trusts abroad—so even if

I wanted to be mercenary, I'd have a hard job to get anything.' Her small hand came up to lightly touch his cheek. 'But why are we having such an awful conversation when there are so many other things to talk about?'

'You're right, sweetheart,' her husband said, and turned to Yorke. 'I'm glad you've got no hard feelings because Anne chose *me*.'

'Why should I have?' Yorke replied. 'Anne and I parted long before she met you.'

'That's true,' Jack Coram agreed. 'You chose one kind of animal and I chose another.' He accompanied his words with a gentle slap on his wife's behind.

'Don't!' she said sharply.

'Sorry, honey.'

'How do you like living in America?' Rowena spoke for the first time, her manner so charmingly gracious that she gave the impression of being the hostess instead of a guest. By comparison with Anne's silver fairness she looked extremely dark, but there was little to choose between the two women when it came to personality, and seeing their glances meet and clash, Beth knew that each one had recognised the mettle of the other. If it came to a fight between them, she would be hard pressed to know which one she would back to win.

'I don't think you can call Texas America,' Anne replied to Rowena's question. 'It's so vast it's almost a country of its own.'

'Don't you ever hanker to live in England?'

'All the time. A day doesn't go by when I wish I could be back there . . .' There was a short silence, though it did not seem to disturb Jack Coram, who merely shrugged and said easily:

'I bet you wouldn't feel the same if you actually had

123

to live in England now. You've been away from it so long that——'

'Only five years.'

'England has changed in that time and so have you. You're a sun-worshipper, honey, and you love the outdoor life.'

'Cornwall isn't the North Pole,' Anne said coolly.

'Maybe not, but there'd be no swimming in your own pool all the year round and no hot desert nights and acres of stillness. You'd get claustrophobia if you were back in your old home.'

'Care to bet on it?'

'That would only make you more obstinately determined to show me how wrong I am.'

Anne shrugged and Beth, watching the couple, was interested in the seemingly effortless way he commanded his wife, though she wondered fleetingly whether he was guided by instinct or calculation. Despite his easy-going manner, he was a difficult man to assess, which was not surprising, she supposed, for anyone who made so much money in a lifetime must be complicated; and lucky too, for that always played a great part in it.

John Stallard strolled over to join them and the conversation moved away from personalities to the basic reason for the Texans' visit. Hiram and Walter Pickard were both in their late fifties; tall, tanned, with thinning blond hair, and were so near in age and alike in appearance that they could have passed for twins. They had focused their attention on Yorke and plied him with so many questions that after a moment he drew them off to one side so that they would not impede the flow of other conversation. But Beth noticed that Anne's eyes kept moving across to him and though she joined in the talk, her manner was distrait, as if she longed to be beside

Yorke and resented anything that prevented her from doing so.

They stood around talking and drinking for an interminable length of time and Beth's head was beginning to ache by the time they went into the dining-room. John Stallard seated everyone himself, placing the Marchioness and Anne on either side of him and Yorke at the other end of the table between Rowena and Beth. Jack Coram was on Beth's other side and, unwilling to look at Yorke, she focused on the Texan, asking him about his life and gradually finding her interest held. He confessed to having had no formal education, but he was well read and knowledgeable about the political and economic situation in Europe, apart from his own country. 'Hiram and Walter are much more insular than I am,' he admitted as she expressed surprise at his acute perception of a current British problem. 'But in my lifetime I've seen the world getting smaller and smaller and it hasn't stopped shrinking yet. If one wants peace, one has to think in global terms and not about one's own little bit of territory.'

'It's a pity your views aren't shared by everyone,' Beth said.

'If they were, I'd have nothing to fight for!'

She laughed. 'You sound as if you like fighting.'

'I do—as long as it's for a good cause. I've made all the money I need, so I have to find something to fight for.'

'I never thought a millionaire ever confessed to having as much money as he needed.'

'How many millionaires do you know?'

'You're the first one.'

'What about Yorke?'

'He isn't a millionaire,' she said quickly.

'According to Anne he has a great estate and enough

paintings to fill a museum. Still, I guess one can't sell heirlooms, so in pure cash terms you might be right.'

'I have every intention of selling my heirlooms.' Yorke's voice told them he had overheard their conversation and Jack Coram leaned forward in order to see him better.

'You mean you would give up your inheritance? I can't believe that.'

'It's true. Powys means a great deal to me, but my research work means considerably more, and if my home has to be sold in order for me to carry on with my work...'

'Well, if Powys comes on the market, don't forget to tell me. It's the one place I know Anne would give her eye teeth to own.'

Beth knew from Yorke's very stillness that he was exercising enormous control over himself. How much it must hurt him to hear Jack Coram make such a remark and why on earth had the Texan been so tactless? She glanced at Jack and saw he was smiling, but a second glance showed her that his hands were clenched tightly around his wine glass. No, whatever one could say about him, one could not describe him as tactless. His remark had been deliberately made to incite. But incite what? Jealousy in Yorke? A row between himself and the young and handsome aristocrat whom he still obviously feared? Yet if he feared him, why had he brought his wife to Mandama?

'If and when I give up Powys,' Yorke answered the Texan's question, 'it will be made over to the National Trust.'

'Don't you have to make provision for the upkeep of it?'

Yorke nodded and looked surprised by the other man's

knowledge. 'That's why I'd sell all the heirlooms that weren't entailed.'

'And put the money into Mandama? If you did that, John Stallard wouldn't need us!'

'I wouldn't use the money here,' Yorke said firmly. 'The research we do at Mandama is only partly in my line. If I had *carte blanche*, I'd engage on one particular field of research only.'

'Rabies is your line, isn't it?'

'Yes, but I'm moving towards the study of the brain.' Yorke hesitated. 'It's a somewhat complicated line.'

Jack Coram sipped his wine. 'Well, as I said before, if you want to give me the opportunity of buying Powys, I'll give you the best price for it. Anne's set her heart on a stately home, and you know what she's like once she wants something.'

Yorke's smile was thin. 'I'd advise you not to give in to her. Once you weaken, you're lost.'

'And you should know, eh?' the Texan quipped. 'The only way you were able to hold out against her was to put five thousand miles between you!'

Yorke coloured and Beth, averting her eyes, noticed that Rowena was looking at him with an expression that could only be described as predatory: a raw hungry look that Yorke seemed suddenly to notice, for he frowned and then spoke to her.

'It must be tedious for you to listen to all this talk about the past. I'm sorry, my dear.'

The remark could not have been more calculated to ease the older girl's mind, for he had subtly indicated that he too found it tedious and this, to Rowena, could only mean that he was more concerned with the future.

'I've always considered it fruitless to look back,' she said loudly. 'Life is for living—and that means action!'

'Surely one can learn from the past,' Beth said impulsively. 'It can often stop you from repeating other people's mistakes.'

'I don't agree,' Jack Coram cut in. 'People generally go on making the same mistakes all their lives.'

'What a depressing thing to believe!' Beth replied.

'There speaks youth!' the Texan grinned. 'Believe me, honey, the older you get, the more you realise we are what we are. Circumstances may alter and they may alter *us* a bit, but intrinsically we remain the same.'

'I agree with Beth.' Yorke came back into the conversation, his voice sharper and less drawling. 'If we never learn from experience—as you seem to believe—then we aren't even as intelligent as most animals!'

'We're probably not!' Jack Coram said. 'That's why I'm all for promoting more research into our own brain power. When you think that we barely utilise half of our brain——' He stopped and looked sheepish. 'Heck—I don't need to tell *you* about the brain!'

'I think you'd be very interested in seeing some of Yorke's recent work,' said Rowena, ignoring the irritable look Yorke gave her. 'If you'd like to come and——'

'John's arranging the itinerary,' Yorke interrupted smoothly. 'I suggest we leave it to him.'

'I'm sure he'd have no objection to my seeing your line of work first,' Jack Coram said. 'Sooner or later I'll be seeing it anyway, so why not sooner?'

Accepting the truth of this, Yorke shrugged, and the Texan, seeing the gesture as a sign of defeat, began to ply both him and Rowena with questions.

Beth leaned back in her chair. Now that talk centred entirely on research, it was safe for her to relax. Only if the conversation swung back to Anne would there be any likelihood of tension. She glanced along the length of the table, not surprised to see that Anne's attention was focused on their end, her eyes resting on Yorke with the same hungry look shown by Rowena. Beth bit back a sigh, wondering how Yorke felt to know he was going to be fought over by two women. Yet neither of them was right for him. Anne had already proved herself fickle and Rowena would be demanding and authoritarian. Yet of the two, the Welsh girl would appreciate his work more. But that was where her understanding ended, for she had little love of heritage and tradition. Life to her was a day-to-day affair, and her desire to cure disease came not so much from her love of humanity but from a dislike of anything that was unsolved. Anne, of course, went to the other extreme. Materialism was the throne at which she worshipped, and because of it she had sacrificed her love for Yorke. But now she regretted this. Her arrival at Mandama made this all too clear. But what did she hope to gain by coming back into his life? Was it to see if he still loved her and to find out if they had a future together? And what would she do when she discovered he still wanted to remain here? Seeing her so well groomed and glittering with diamonds, it was hard to imagine her giving up her life of luxury. Yet she was sufficiently subtle to try and get the best of both worlds, providing Yorke was still a willing victim.

'I thought you were interested in rabies?' Anne's voice, clear as a bell, caused everyone at the table to fall quiet, and made it impossible for Yorke not to answer her.

'So I was to begin with,' he said, 'but over the years my interest changed.'

'Then why do you still stay at Mandama?' she asked. 'I mean, you can study the brain anywhere in the world.'

'The two best research centres for that are here and in America.'

'Then you should go to America. It's far more civilised than——' Anne stopped, embarrassed. 'Forgive me, Dr Stallard, it was a thoughtless thing to say.'

'But true. We can't compete with the United States when it comes to amenities. What you say about Yorke is perfectly correct.'

'Then what keeps you here?' Anne returned to the attack on Yorke.

'Because I am allowed to follow my own line of research. In other places I would have to follow work already in progress.'

'Unless you had your *own* research centre.'

Yorke's eyes narrowed into glittering slits. 'That would take a substantial amount of money.'

'Why not sell Powys instead of giving it away?'

'I still wouldn't have what I need. A research centre requires money the whole time.'

'Then be nice to Jack. I'm sure he can help you.'

'We are all being nice to him.'

Yorke's smile was strained and Anne, realising it was unwise to push the conversation any further in the direction she wanted, turned back to her host. The conversation became general again, with Rowena talking to the other two Texans and Jack Coram once again discussing the state of the world with Beth. It was a relief to her when they finally left the dining-room, and murmuring an excuse she went to the bedroom which had been set aside for the ladies and remained there until she felt everyone had re-settled themselves, hoping she would then be able to return and choose her own seat as far from Yorke as possible. She brushed her hair, dissatisfied with her appearance. How faded she looked compared with Anne! The door behind her opened and the woman in her thoughts became a reality.

'So this is where you've been hiding?' Anne said, sitting on a stool and tipping the contents of her handbag on to the top of the dressing-table. There was a beautiful lace handkerchief, a gold and diamond compact and lipstick case, and a small gold comb. 'Yorke gave me that,' Anne pointed to the comb. 'Pretty, isn't it? I always carry it with me.'

'For sentimental reasons?' Beth asked stiffly, knowing she was expected to say something.

'Of course. Yorke is the only man I've ever been sentimental about.' Anne picked up her lipstick and applied it to her mouth. Her lips, Beth saw, were not as full as they seemed, and owed their curves more to artifice than to nature.

'How long have you known him?' Anne continued. 'He introduced you as a friend of the family, but I gather you're the Marchioness's companion.'

'Yes, I am,' Beth said bluntly, 'and I met him for the first time when I came out here—which was two weeks ago.'

Anne's head lifted and their eyes met in the mirror. She had grey eyes like Beth, but they were a lighter, more silvery grey. 'How odd of Yorke to suggest you were a friend. I suppose he was trying to make you feel at home. He has always been very kind.'

'So has the Marchioness.'

'That old bag!' Anne said viciously. 'She was delighted when I left Yorke. She never made any secret of her dislike of me.' The blonde head tilted. 'I suppose you know all about it? You couldn't work for her and not know!'

'We do not discuss you,' Beth said composedly.

Anne laughed suddenly. 'You're very diplomatic for a companion.'

'Companions have to be—if they don't want to get fired!'

'You obviously don't. Still, I suppose as far as jobs go, yours must be quite good. Living at Powys makes up for a lot.' The lipstick clattered to the mirrored top. 'I love that house. From the time I was a child I made up my mind to live there. If Yorke hadn't been so damned obstinate I'd be there with him now.'

'At least you and the Marchioness have Powys in common,' Beth made a tentative move to the door, but she knew she could not walk out without being rude.

'According to her, we had nothing in common,' Anne retorted. 'She loves Powys because it means the family. I love it because I see it as the right background for me.' The lipstick was put away and the powder compact opened. 'Living in Texas is like living on a gold bar. You enjoy it, but you can't grow roots on a gold bar!'

'Your husband doesn't give the impression of being rootless.'

'Don't let looks fool you. He would like to have a traditional background just as much as I would. God, if only I had my life again!' The compact clattered to the mirror top too and Anne banged one clenched fist against the other. 'What stupid mistakes we make when we're young!'

Beth did not know what to say. Everything she was now hearing only added to her sense of impending disaster. Jack Coram might well covet the same background as his wife, but Anne also included Yorke in hers. But surely the Texan had known this when he had agreed to come here?

'Yorke's relationship with Rowena Vale,' Anne was

speaking again, her face sharp with dislike. 'What is it?'

'They're colleagues.'

'She's in love with him,' Anne said bluntly, 'but I don't think he's in love with *her*. In fact, I'm sure he isn't.' Again Beth said nothing, but this time her silence was not allowed to go unnoticed. 'What do you think? You're as aware of him as I am.'

'Yorke's emotional life is not my concern.'

'Don't come Little Miss Prissy with me,' Anne sparkled angrily. 'You're as much in love with him as I am.'

'If you'll excuse me, I'll go for my coffee.' Beth went to open the door, but found her way barred by Anne Coram, who had moved across the room with the swiftness of a cheetah.

'There's no reason to get upset because you love him,' she said. 'You're in good company. Most women love Yorke. The trouble is he doesn't love *them*. I was the only one he ever wanted.' Anne's voice grew softer. 'And he still wants me. I saw it in the way he looked at me; the way he dropped my hand as if he were afraid to touch it.'

'I would rather you didn't make me your confidant, Mrs Coram.' Beth spoke from between stiff lips.

'Does it hurt you to think of him with another woman?' Anne asked, giving Beth the full battery of her eyes. 'You look remarkably like me, you know. I wouldn't be surprised if that was why the Marchioness engaged you. From her point of view you would make the ideal wife for Yorke. A docile little nonentity who would let her continue to rule Powys the way she has ruled it all her life. If I had married Yorke, I would have made her leave.'

'I'm sure she wouldn't have wanted to stay,' Beth said.

'It's so clear to me,' Anne muttered, as if she had not heard Beth's comment. 'She brought you out here in the hope that Yorke would fall for you. I mean, if he couldn't have me, give him a copy instead!'

'As you seem to have worked everything out so clearly ...' Beth made to push past her, but Anne still did not move out of the way.

'You don't stand a chance of getting him,' Anne continued. 'Yorke still loves *me*. Not that he'll admit it, as long as I'm married to Jack. He has always had very rigid principles.'

'I'm sure you haven't.'

'How right you are,' Anne said goodhumouredly. 'I don't see any problems in the future. Jack loves me too much to stand in the way of my happiness, and he knows I've never forgotten Yorke.'

'Shouldn't you be telling this to him and not me?'

'You were here,' Anne shrugged, 'and I had to talk to someone. I'm not scared of you,' she added. 'It's Rowena Vale I don't like.'

'As you're so sure Yorke still loves you,' Beth could not help saying, 'I'm surprised you let any woman bother you.'

'Yorke has principles,' Anne repeated. 'And getting engaged to Rowena might just strike him as the obvious thing to do.'

With an exclamation Beth pushed Anne aside and reached for the door handle. The woman made no attempt to stop her and Beth flung open the door and ran into the hall. Anne Coram's determination to discard her husband and take another man was sickening, not only in its disregard of promises made, but of loyalty and morality too. Yet it also showed how obsessively she still wanted Yorke, and this made her marriage to Jack

Coram incomprehensible. Surely it would have been preferable for her to have lived in Mandama with the man she loved rather than live in Texas with a man who meant nothing to her? Yet obviously at the time Anne had not thought so, and it had taken her five years to discover it for herself. Five years in which Yorke had remained unmarried. No wonder Anne was confident she would be able to get him back; it did not look as if she had ever lost him.

CHAPTER TEN

BETH's sleep that night was haunted by a vivid dream of Yorke running across a bare landscape pursued by a crowd of wild animals. At the base of a fever tree two of them caught him and started to pull him in different directions. In front of her anguished eyes he began to disintegrate as though he were a piece of wool slowly being unravelled. The horror of it was so intense that she was rendered powerless to cry out, and only as she finally found her voice and started to scream, did she wake up.

The lemon light of dawn was seeping into the room and, still trembling violently, she sat up, knowing this was the only way to completely dispel the horror of her subconscious thoughts. It did not require much imagination to see the nightmare for what it was. The two animals who had fought over Yorke were Rowena and Anne, each of whom wanted him for different reasons, and each of whom would—in their own way—destroy him; Anne because she did not love him and only wanted him because she had not yet managed to conquer him, and Rowena who would encourage him to turn his back on the past because she believed this was the only way she stood a chance of having a future with him.

Restlessly Beth pushed aside her covering sheet. She was reluctant to start dressing in case the noise of her shower disturbed the Marchioness, yet it was impossible to remain in bed, and she compromised by having a quick wash, donned jeans and a cotton top and slipped out of the rondavel in search of a secluded corner where she could walk over the dew-wet grass and try to come to terms with her unease. There was a quiet stretch of land at the back of Yorke's laboratories, and she made her way towards it, so deep in thought that she did not see the man coming towards her until she knocked into him. The aroma of after-shave lotion—musky and disturbing—told her it was the one man she did not wish to see alone, but it was too late to do anything about it, and with lids half-lowered to veil her eyes she raised her head, bade him good morning, and went to walk past. Resolutely he barred her way, the slight smile on the corners of his mouth telling her he knew of her reluctance to talk to him.

'You're up early, Beth.'

'So are you.'

'But I'm not on holiday.'

'Neither am I. I'm here as your grandmother's companion.'

The smile left his face. 'What am I supposed to deduce from that comment?'

'Nothing.' She tried again to walk past him, but he turned and kept in step with her.

'Why are you annoyed with me?' he asked. 'And don't bother to deny it, because it's written all over your face. Is it something I've done or something I *haven't* done?'

'I'd rather not talk about it.'

'Maybe you wouldn't, but I have no intention of remaining in ignorance. Come on, Beth, out with it.'

'Don't you know,' she cried in exasperation, 'or did you think I'd be flattered for you to introduce me last night as a friend of the family? I'm not ashamed of working for my living, you know.'

'I never thought you were.' He stopped and caught her arm. 'I didn't do it for that reason, Beth. Please believe me.'

She shrugged as if to dismiss the subject and took a tentative step forward, hoping he would not choose to follow her. But still he kept pace with her, matching his long, loping stride to her shorter, quicker one.

'You made a hit with Coram last night,' he went on. 'He was pretty taken with you.'

'All I did was listen to him,' she stated. 'Men like that.'

'You talked to him too, and he enjoyed it.' Yorke's words implied that he had been watching her and Beth felt a tremor of pleasure which died as he added: 'Anne wasn't overjoyed to see her husband paying you so much attention.'

'She has nothing to fear from any woman,' Beth said shortly. 'Mr Coram dotes on her—as I'm sure you've seen for yourself.'

'Yes, I have—and it makes for various problems.'

She quickened her pace. 'I'm not interested in them.'

'That's a pity, because I was hoping you would help me with them.' He glanced at his watch. 'Seven in the morning isn't the best time to have this kind of conversation, but we don't seem to have any option. Will you have breakfast with me, Beth? What I have to say to you is best said on a full stomach.'

Mystified, she nodded and allowed him to lead her forward. Expecting to be taken to the dining-hall, she was discomfited to find him making for the rondavel where he lived. As he reached the door and went to unlock it, he saw the look on her face and gave her a sharp smile.

'I have no designs on your virtue, Beth. I want to talk

to you alone and this is the only place where I can do it in reasonable comfort.'

Tight-lipped, she followed him into a small, austerely furnished bedsitting-room which had already been tidied after the night. Two cups stood on a small table and beside them an electric coffee pot was percolating.

'I have cream crackers and biscuits in the refrigerator,' he said, pointing to a small one by the wall, 'but if you want anything else I'll get one of the boys to bring it over from the dining-room.'

The thought of food nauseated her and she shook her head. Silently he motioned her to sit down and then prepared the coffee. It was strong and aromatic and she sipped it with real pleasure. Yorke did not sit down but, cup in hand, went to stand by the window. The curtains had been drawn, but blinds were tilted to keep out most of the sunlight and they cast bars of shadow across his face, making him look like a prisoner. His voice held the same restrained quality and was clipped as though he had rehearsed what he was now saying.

'After the party broke up last night, Jack Coram stayed on talking to John and myself. He made it clear that he prefers my own line of research to any of the other work being done here.'

'John must have been disappointed,' Beth murmured.

'Not as much as he would have been if he hadn't already got the promise of half a million dollars from the Pollock brothers.'

'That's wonderful,' she exclaimed.

'I thought you'd be pleased. You like Stallard, don't you?'

She nodded silently and there was a momentary pause before Yorke resumed speaking.

'Coram is willing to put up five million dollars to start the Coram Institute for Neurological Research. He would like me to run it.'

Beth was not sure what to say. This was everything Yorke had been working towards, yet she was not sure how he felt at receiving such an offer from the man who was husband of the woman he still loved. For he did still love Anne; of that she was sure.

'Well, Beth,' he went on, 'don't you think that's wonderful news too?'

'Of course. It's everything you want.'

'Everything,' he echoed. 'The trouble is, do I want it from Coram?'

'Because he's Anne's husband?'

The lift of the wide shoulders gave her the answer she had expected. 'And that isn't the whole of it either,' he added. 'Coram feels that since he'll be putting up the money for an entirely new project, he'd like to have it sited somewhere else.' There was a pause, longer than the first one and more significant. 'Anne suggested it should be in England.'

'At Powys, I assume,' Beth said in a lifeless voice.

Yorke looked surprised. 'You know?'

'Call it an inspired guess.'

'I see. I thought she had mentioned it to you. You were both out of the room a long time together.'

Again his comment showed that he had noticed all Anne's movements last night, and Beth wondered if she would ever reach the stage in her life when what he did or felt about another woman would no longer hurt her. 'We didn't discuss that particular subject,' she said. 'Mrs Coram was more concerned to tell me how much she regretted not marrying you.'

'Anne always loves being dramatic in front of an

140

audience,' he said dryly. 'And I daresay you made an ideal one for her, staring at her all big-eyed and innocent.'

'I was staring at her with curiosity,' Beth asserted. 'Everyone keeps telling me I look like her and——'

'A superficial resemblance only,' he cut in, and catching hold of her wrist, drew her to her feet. 'Why are you on the defensive with me, Beth? I need your help and when you behave in this way, I don't find it easy to ask you.'

'My help?' Her embarrassment dissolved beneath her surprise. 'Help in what?'

'Can't you guess? You saw Anne's behaviour last night, and she made it plain to you that she wants me and doesn't care how much she hurts Coram in the process.'

'And you don't want Coram to be hurt.' It was a statement, not a question, for if the Texan was willing to finance Yorke, then the least Yorke could do in return was not to take away his wife.

'Of course I don't want to hurt Coram!' Yorke burst out. 'Nor do I want to encourage Anne. If I'd known how she was going to behave, I would have gone away while she was here.'

'It's a good thing you didn't,' Beth asserted, 'or you wouldn't have received Coram's offer.'

'I may still not accept it,' he said quietly. 'Unless you're willing to help me.'

She pulled her hand away from his and sat down again. She was aware of Yorke watching her but refused to look at him, not knowing what she would see on his face but certain of what he would see on hers. Fixedly she stared at the coffee cup on the small table.

'What you're trying to say,' she said in a matter-of-fact way, 'is that if you take Jack Coram's money, you can't take his wife.'

'Yes.'

'And you want the money more?'

'I wouldn't put it like that.'

'Don't quibble!' she said sharply. 'What I've said is the truth. You want to make Mrs Coram think you're in love with someone else so that she'll stay with her husband.'

'Yes,' Yorke said slowly. 'Does that mean the answer is yes?'

'I'm sure it will be. I can't imagine Rowena turning you down.'

'Rowena?' For an instant, Yorke looked blank, then his mouth curved into a thin, tight line. 'Are you suggesting I become engaged to Rowena?'

Beth began to shake. 'Isn't that what you meant?'

'You don't think I'm crazy enough to jump out of the frying pan into the fire, do you?' Anger hardened his voice. 'Because I can't see a future with Anne it doesn't mean I can see one with Rowena!'

'But you liked her and——'

'I like a lot of women,' he interrupted, 'but I wouldn't want to marry them. As a wife, Rowena would be impossible!'

'But it's only a temporary arrangement.' Even as she heard herself speak, Beth knew the impossibility of what she was suggesting. Rowena wanted Yorke permanently, and even if she agreed to a false engagement she would do her best to make it a real one.

'You see?' Yorke said humorously. 'Even you know it wouldn't work with Rowena. No, my dear, it's you or no one.'

Had she not been sitting down, Beth would have fallen, for at Yorke's words all the strength left her limbs. How stupid of her not to have recognised that this was what Yorke had been leading up to saying. Who better to help him out of an awkward situation than his grandmother's colourless little companion?

'Well, Beth,' he said, 'will you help me?'

'What will happen if I don't?'

'I'll try to keep Anne off my neck for as long as I can. But Coram is no fool. He'll soon guess what's on her mind.'

'Don't you think he already knows?' Beth asked. 'Surely that's why he made you that offer. It's a test of your integrity.'

Yorke frowned. 'You may well be right,' he said. 'If you are, then Coram is more subtle than I realised. But he's still taking a gamble. How does he know I won't accept his offer and then, when it's been finalised, run off with his wife?'

'He's a better judge of character than you are,' Beth said coldly. 'He knows you wouldn't do that.'

'Anne would. She has no scruples when it comes to something she wants.' His frown deepened. 'If she sees she isn't getting anywhere with me, she might well try and make Coram change his mind about the grant.'

'Poor Yorke, you really are between the devil and the deep blue sea! You want to stop Coram from seeing you as his rival and you have to reject Anne without hurting her pride too much—hence your pretended engagement to me—which Anne will immediately know is a joke.'

'You put it in harsh terms.'

'I'm putting it truthfully. Do you think your engagement to me will worry the beautiful Anne Coram? Or

143

do you just want her to stop thinking of you as husband material and see you only as a lover?'

'I don't want Anne as a wife *or* a mistress,' he said loudly, 'though for some reason I can't fathom you still refuse to believe me. But I do want the Coram Institute! And the only way I can get it is to make Anne believe I'm in love with someone else.'

'It was clever of you to think of me. At least you can be sure I won't want you on a permanent basis!'

'You are making that more clear with every word,' he said harshly. 'I hadn't realised how much you dislike me.'

'My feelings are not as insipid as my looks.'

He flung out one hand in a disclaiming gesture. 'Insipid is the last word I'd use to describe you. You're fire and ice, Beth—at the moment, more fire than anything else.'

'Justice,' she said coldly.

'Fire,' he reiterated, and pulling her up once more, abruptly lowered his head and covered her mouth with his own.

She tried to resist its pressure, but there was a ruthlessness in him that had not been there before, and her struggles only succeeded in making his hands dig more fiercely into her shoulders.

'No, you don't,' he grated. 'If it's home truths you want, you're going to hear a few from me, my prim and proper Beth Miller!'

Tightening his grip, he pushed her backwards against the divan. As the edge of it caught the back of her legs, she toppled and fell. Before she could rise, the weight of his body was upon her, causing her to sink deeper into the mattress, unable to move and not even wanting to

144

do so. The treacherous languor of her body could not be denied and served to increase her awareness of him, making her conscious of the thudding of his heart and the pressure of his chest upon her breasts. His face was so near it was almost out of focus and she closed her eyes, frightened in case he saw the love in them.

'Do I repel you so much that you can't even pretend to be in love with me?' he questioned huskily. 'I thought you would have jumped at the chance.'

'I'll jump at the chance never to see you again!'

'Think it over,' he taunted. 'An innocent companion, untouched by man, turning down the opportunity of becoming engaged to a Marquis!'

'And then being jilted by him when she's served her purpose,' Beth flared.

'How can you be sure of that? If you play your cards properly, you may be kept on permanently! At least it would make my grandmother happy.'

The thought of the Marchioness robbed Beth of the major force of her anger and for the first time she appreciated all that Jack Coram's offer could mean, no longer seeing it as a carrot which Anne had encouraged him to dangle in front of Yorke's eyes, but as the beginning of a situation which would enable Yorke to pursue his own life as well as carry on the traditions of his forefathers.

Aware that she had become quiescent beneath him, Yorke raised himself to look more clearly into her face. 'You're thinking of my grandmother,' he said, guessing her thoughts.

'Yes,' she admitted. 'If you built the Institute at Powys and came back there, it would give her a new lease of life.'

'Then help me over the next few weeks.'

'It will take much longer than that.'

'No, it won't. Once everything is signed, Anne and Coram will go back to the States.'

Beth hesitated, unable to believe that things would work out the way Yorke anticipated. She could not see Anne believing in the truth of his engagement or accepting it, yet if Yorke thought otherwise, why shouldn't she do as he asked? At least for a few weeks she would be able to pretend he loved her and enjoy a happiness she might never have again.

'Very well,' she whispered. 'I'll do it for your grandmother's sake.'

'Not for mine?'

'Why should I care about a man who can only run away from one woman by hiding behind the skirts of another?'

'And most unwilling skirts at that,' he mocked, and lowering his face to hers, began to kiss her with increasing passion.

Pride made her refuse to fight him and she lay passive as a doll, forcing back the treacherous emotions that invaded her at his touch. She tried to concentrate on the things she could see: the whitewashed walls, the woven curtains at the window, the light on the ceiling; but all she was aware of was Yorke's quick breathing and the thick dark hair that fell forward and brushed against her skin. The desire she was striving to deny began to reassert itself, and the urge to put up her arms and clasp hold of him was so great that she gave a gasping cry. Hearing it, he lifted himself away from her and stared at her with a look she could not fathom. 'What sort of man do you want, Beth? Women don't usually find me as uninspiring as you obviously do.'

'You sound as if you've gone around experimenting.'

'I tried hard to forget Anne,' he said.

'And didn't succeed,' Beth wanted to say, but held back the words. Nevertheless they lay heavy between them and he scowled as he spoke.

'Are you worried about hurting Stallard? Is that why you didn't want to help me?'

'That was one of the reasons,' she lied, seizing on John as an excuse. 'I'm very fond of him.'

'You hardly know him.'

'You hardly know me,' she replied, 'yet you believe you understand me.'

'You're different.' His tone was curt. 'You are as transparent as glass.'

The irony of his remark made her smile and he gave an exasperated sound and stood up. 'What's funny about that?'

'If I'm so transparent, surely you don't need me to tell you!'

Taking the point, he gave another irritated mutter, and resisting the urge to confound him with the truth, Beth too jumped up from the divan. Her shoes had fallen off and she felt even smaller beside him, the tip of her head barely reaching his shoulder.

'Such a little thing but so much content,' he said. 'I envy the man who will eventually get it.'

Hurriedly she glanced at her wrist watch. It was eight o'clock and the camp would already be astir. 'Will we tell your grandmother the truth about us?' she asked, not looking at him.

'I don't want anyone to know—not even Stallard.'

Beth was glad of this, for it would at least keep John out of her way for the rest of her stay here. But she was less happy at the prospect of deceiving her employer.

'If my grandmother knows our engagement isn't genuine,' he explained, acknowledging that he understood how she felt on this point, 'she may worry about giving herself away, and that would put an unnecessary strain on her.'

His justification for secrecy was too logical to be rejected, and she nodded in silence.

'Don't look so worried,' he continued sarcastically. 'I promise not to be a demanding lover!'

'No lover at all,' she snapped. 'If you try to kiss me again, I—I——'

'Might respond to me?' he cut in.

'I'll give you back your ring,' she cried, and then stopped, colour flooding into her face as she realised she had none to give him.

'I must remedy that,' he said, reading her thoughts, and taking the signet ring off his little finger, caught hold of her hand and slipped on the ring.

It was too large but not uncomfortably so, and she stared down at it, overcome by a mixture of sensations that robbed her of all speech. If only their engagement was genuine and she could raise her head and see true affection in his dark eyes. If only her future really lay at Powys and she could look forward to sharing the years with this man. If only ... Two small words that reminded her she was an actress playing a part—as Yorke was playing his.

'I'll give you a diamond ring when we return home,' he said.

'By that time our engagement will be over.'

'How remiss of me to forget!' Moving to the door, he half opened it. 'Shall we go and break the news to our loved ones, *darling?*'

'By all means.' Beth's head lifted sharply. 'Dearest,' she added as she walked past him, and saw the answering glint in his eyes. Their engagement was a pretence, but it looked as if it would hold some moments of genuine emotion—albeit they would be stormy ones.

CHAPTER ELEVEN

THE Marchioness made no secret of her delight at Yorke's engagement and within half an hour was happily envisaging a new life for Powys, with the rooms ringing with the sound of children's voices and her grandson firmly ensconced in the family seat. So great became Beth's guilt at the lie she was living that when she saw Yorke later that day, she pleaded with him to tell his grandmother the truth.

'I daren't do it now,' he said firmly. 'She would be so distressed to find out it wasn't true that she'd unwittingly give the game away.'

'Don't you have any conscience about deceiving her?'

'Not when I think of the future. Or would you rather we ran the risk of Coram withdrawing his offer?'

She gave an angry exclamation. 'Which do you care about most? The chance of having your own research centre or being able to return to Powys?'

His answer was so long coming that she thought he was not going to make one, and she was surprised when he swung round on the bench on which they were sitting—they were in a cool patch of land behind the rondavel—and said explosively:

'I'm not as uncaring for Powys as you think. But when you can't have something you make yourself believe you don't want it. That's how it has been with Powys.'

'Nothing stopped you from living there,' she reminded him.

'Only my conscience. I had to give in to it even though

it meant living miles away from everything I wanted—including the woman I loved.'

Beyond the path of shadow the bright sun shone as brightly as before, yet to Beth it seemed to grow dimmer, made so by Yorke's words, which sent everything into a lower key. Sensing her change of mood, Yorke stirred restlessly beside her, his eyes staring broodingly at some insects busily marching across the grass. His preoccupation gave her a chance to study him, and she feasted her eyes on his black hair, noting that there was not one strand of grey in it, and his wide, sloping shoulders, their strong muscles visible beneath the thin silk of his white shirt. How strong he was despite his slimness! How strong and yet how weak when it came to women. She sighed. At least to one particular woman, who still had the power to affect him so deeply that the only way he could prevent himself from doing what she wanted was to pretend he was in love with another girl.

'My father died of a kidney ailment which today would never have killed him,' Yorke said suddenly. 'I was six at the time.'

'I had the impression his death was an accident.'

'Only inasmuch as it could have been prevented if he'd had the proper treatment. My grandmother rarely speaks of it because I don't think she has ever recovered from the blow.'

'Is that the reason you went in for research, instead of general medicine?'

'Probably. But ever since I can remember I wanted to find out why things happened and how they could be prevented.'

'When did your mother die?' Beth asked, her curiosity fully aroused.

'When I was three. Also from an illness that five years

later became curable. I was brought up by the same nurse who had looked after my father,' he added.

Beth had a vision of a dark-haired little boy surrounded by elderly people and yearning for the parents he could barely remember.

'I wasn't lonely and I enjoyed my own company,' Yorke informed her, his comment illustrating his ability to read her thoughts. 'I loved the countryside and I was crazy about animals. I practically had a menagerie of my own.'

'I'm surprised you didn't become a vet!'

'I prefer to help people.' He looked her fully in the face. 'I don't know why I'm boring you with my past, except that I'm trying to make you understand why my work is important to me.'

'I am not concerned with its importance to *you*.' Her voice was colder than she had meant it to be, so intent was she on not letting him know that she had found his reasons moving. 'I am concerned only with your grandmother.'

'Yes,' he sighed, 'you've made that pretty clear already.' One dark brow lifted. 'When we first met I had the impression you didn't find me repugnant. But now ... Is it something I have done or haven't I grown on you?'

It was a question he had asked her before and she was surprised that he should still be curious as to the answer. But then perhaps Yorke Powys, last in line of an illustrious family, was not used to having women remain aloof to him.

'Answer me, Beth,' he said.

'I don't dislike you, Yorke. I just find you——' She paused, then found what she hoped was an excellent reason. 'I have never felt comfortable with men of my own generation. I prefer them to be older.'

'Like John Stallard,' he said coldly.

'Yes. Like John.'

'But for the moment you are engaged to me, so you'd do well to forget him.'

'Why should I? Our engagement is only a pretence. If I want to think of another man, I will!'

'Then try and think of one now.'

Before she could stop him, he caught her close and pressed a hard kiss on her parted lips. Even his brief touch set her pulses hammering and the sun around her shimmered as he drew back as a technician walked past. The man stopped to speak and Beth took the opportunity of slipping away.

She was nearly at her rondavel when a slim figure in white glided towards her across the grass.

'Hello there,' said Anne. 'I hear I owe you congratulations. You're a quick worker.'

'You've heard?' Beth said awkwardly.

'The whole camp is buzzing with the news—and astonished by its suddenness.'

'It wasn't sudden to us,' Beth said composedly.

'Really?' Anne's pale grey eyes widened and then narrowed, like a cat stalking its prey. 'Last night neither of you gave any inkling that you were in love. At least Yorke didn't, though you weren't such a good actress.'

'And now I needn't act any longer,' Beth replied.

'Only for the time being.'

'The time being mine,' said Beth, and went to move on.

'Don't count your chickens yet,' Anne Coram spat out the words. 'Yorke only became engaged to you because you remind him of me. He's using you as his defence—

nothing more than that! I can take him away from you any time I like.'

'Then what's stopping you?'

'My husband's money. Not that I need it for myself,' she added delicately. 'He has already given me more than enough to keep me happy for the rest of my life. But I wouldn't have enough to buy Yorke the toys he wants to play with. Research establishments come pretty expensive these days. But once he and Jack have settled things...' Her eyes widened and narrowed again. 'Make the most of your time with Yorke. I can promise you it won't last long.'

Beth longed to push past Anne Coram and close the door in her face. But a pride she had never known she possessed kept her where she was. She was sure Yorke had not given Anne any indication of the way he still felt about her, and though the older girl might assume the engagement to be a pretence, she had no proof of it.

'No matter what you believe, Mrs Coram, Yorke and I are in love and are going to get married.'

Anne Coram gave a tinkling laugh. 'You're a better actress than I gave you credit for, but you still can't fool me. When I'm ready to take Yorke away from you, he'll come running. Remember that, my little carbon copy.' Pale eyes raked her, and had they had the power to do so, would have left weals on Beth's body. 'And also remember that every time he kisses you, he's making believe it's me. That should take away some of your pleasure!'

'Luckily it won't,' Beth managed to say, and this time not even pride could make her continue the conversation. Silently she skirted past the woman, opened the door of her rondavel and closed it quietly behind her.

Only then did she realise she was shaking, and she sank down on the bed and waited for it to pass. How marvellous to be so confident in your power that you believed you could let a man down and still have him come running when you wanted him back. It was an attitude she herself would never feel—least of all with Yorke, whose astringent personality eroded any confidence she had.

Standing up to change into another dress—this one was already damp—she glimpsed her face in the mirror. Eyes sparkling with tears and cheeks flushed with temper, she looked animated enough to fight for any man. Yet looks were deceptive, as she knew too well. 'I *am* just a carbon copy of Anne,' she admitted. 'And a faded one at that!'

Where Anne Coram had expressed disbelief in Yorke's engagement, Rowena—when told of it—expressed incredulity.

'It won't work out,' she stated bluntly when she was momentarily alone with Beth in a corner of John Stallard's living-room, the Director having hurriedly arranged a cocktail party to celebrate his assistant's engagement.

'You and Mrs Coram should get together,' said Beth. 'She is also trying to make herself believe Yorke doesn't love me.'

'Of course he doesn't love you! He was turning to me before you came here and he'll turn back to me when you leave.'

'When I leave Mandama, Yorke will come with me,' Beth replied, hoping she was speaking the truth and looking past Rowena's shoulder for a sight of him. He was in the far corner of the room, his profile to her and seemingly with no idea that she desperately wanted him

155

to come and rescue her. Almost as if her need of him had been an audible signal, he turned and searched for her, moving slowly across the floor in her direction.

'You can give Yorke nothing,' Rowena went on bitterly. 'At least Anne has beauty, but *you*——'

'And what do you have?' Beth asked, trying to see the humour of the situation, but failing. So many women all wanting Yorke and only she herself in whom he had sufficient confidence to turn to for protection.

'I can give him intelligence and appreciation of his work. I know the real Yorke, not the outward trappings of an aristocrat. He's a brilliant man and he must be allowed to do the research he wants.'

Rowena's face was mottled red with anger, her bitterness detracting from her vibrant beauty.

Yorke, approaching them, must have noticed it too, for an expression of distaste flitted across his features. 'Aren't you going to congratulate me on my charming fiancée?' he asked with astonishing aplomb.

'I'm not crazy! You're a fool, Yorke, but I know the reason for it.'

'Then you're a jump ahead of me, my dear.' He put an arm along Beth's shoulders and pulled her close. She felt the warmth of his body through his jacket and wondered if he could feel the warmth of her own. He must have felt her trembling, for his hold tightened and he gave her a sudden warm smile. 'Poor darling,' he said tenderly, 'you must feel shattered at the animosity you've aroused.'

'Flattered, not shattered,' Beth said, making an effort to smile back at him. 'It's nice for a girl to know so many women envy her.'

'I don't envy you,' Rowena intervened. 'You're living

in a fool's paradise, and when you wake up you're going to feel an even bigger fool!'

'I suggest you spread your charm among the other guests, Rowena,' Yorke said in the same easy tones he had employed since joining them. 'Otherwise I might forget I'm a gentleman and shut your mouth forcibly.'

Rowena gasped and turned scarlet. 'You know how I feel about you,' she choked. 'I never pretended. I gave you the honour of not lying to you.'

'It was an honour I reciprocated,' he said quietly. 'And I made it extremely clear how I felt about you.'

'Oh, you were the perfect gentleman,' she retorted, 'but it didn't stop you from seeing me all the time.'

'Since we work together, I could hardly have avoided you.'

'You know what I mean,' she said harshly.

'So much so that I can't overlook it. We've worked well together, Rowena. I'm sorry it has to end like this.'

Only then did Beth feel any sympathy for the Welsh girl, for as quickly as the colour had come to her cheeks, it left them, leaving her skin waxy grey.

'You don't mean we ... But I've always worked with you. We're a team.'

'Not once I leave here.'

'You can't dismiss me. John won't let you.'

'I'm not dismissing you from here, Rowena. In fact there's every likelihood that John will offer you my position when he knows you'll be staying on at Mandama.'

'A carrot for the donkey,' Rowena said under her breath. 'You're a clever, scheming man, Yorke. I never guessed it until now.'

Swinging round, she wandered away to where John Stallard was talking to Jack and Anne Coram. The tall, grey-haired Director looked at her with surprise as she moved closer to him and slipped her arm through his.

Beth gave a sigh of relief which Yorke, hearing, mis-interpreted.

'I'm sorry about this, Beth. By the time you're free to tell Stallard the truth about us, it might be too late.'

Deliberately Beth did not correct his assumption. 'Then let me tell him the truth now.'

'No,' he said instantly. 'You gave me your promise you wouldn't.' He glanced again at the older man. 'Any-way, he isn't your type.'

'Who is?' she burst out.

'For the time being I am.' His arm was still about her shoulders, making her conscious that she was backed up against a corner of the wall and sheltered from the rest of the room by an enormous rubber plant.

'Please don't,' she whispered.

'Don't what?' he asked jerkily.

'Don't kiss me again.'

'It was the last thing I had in mind.' He went to step back from her, but before he could move, Jack Coram's voice made him stop.

'So this is where the two of you are hiding. Taking advantage of the greenery, eh?'

Yorke stepped to one side but still kept his arm round Beth. Anne Coram stood beside her husband, a picture of elegance in black chiffon, the diamonds round her throat weighing more than the material itself.

'It seems I'm instrumental in getting you two off to a good start.' Jack Coram gripped Beth's hand and squeezed it. 'Yorke told me you wouldn't marry him until he went back home.'

'That isn't quite how I put it,' Yorke said smoothly. 'Beth merely indicated that she would prefer me to settle in England.'

'Well, either way, this little lady got you to do what Anne couldn't.'

Beth tensed, unsure if the Texan knew on what thin ice he was treading. But he appeared oblivious of the furious look his wife cast him; oblivious too of the smile that sat stiffly on Yorke's face, as if he found the conversation embarrassing.

'When are you planning to return to England?' Jack Coram asked. 'If you're going soon, I'd like to come and pay you a visit.'

'I shall be returning home with Beth and my grandmother,' Yorke said, and as Beth looked at him in astonishment, he nodded. 'John has been kind enough to let me go as soon as I wish.'

'I doubt if it was kindness,' the Texan said dryly, 'so much as a little arm-twisting from the Pickards. They know I'm anxious to get started with the Coram Institute and that means the quicker you're free, the quicker we can work things out.'

'I'm beginning to see what it means to have a Texan godfather,' Yorke drawled.

'I haven't even begun yet.' Jack Coram grinned. 'Wait till we get down to equipment. I want the best that money can buy. The sooner the Coram Institute comes up with a cure for something, the better I'll be pleased!'

'That isn't only a question of the best equipment,' Yorke warned. 'Men have always been more important than the machines they operate.'

'Maybe so, but the best brains can't succeed if they don't have the proper resources. And that's what I aim to provide.' Coram looked at his wife. 'Anne and I will come down to Cornwall with our architect and——'

'Do you have one already?' Yorke asked in astonishment.

'Sure. And he's the best man in his field.'

'Jack always has the best,' Anne drawled. 'It's what he uses his money for.'

'It bought me you, honey, so don't knock the product!'

'You'll stay at Powys, of course,' Yorke put in hastily.

'If you're sure it's no trouble,' said Coram. 'We'll want to take a good look at the estate before we decide where to site the Institute.'

'As far from the house as possible,' Anne said.

'I thought of building in the copse.' Yorke spoke to her directly. 'That way the trees would screen the Institute from the house.'

'What a wonderful idea, darling.' Anne slipped her arm through his. 'It's incredible to think you're going back home again.'

'And all because of me,' her husband reminded her. 'Don't let it give you ideas, honey. I know you left Yorke because he wouldn't live in his home, but now he's going back with a wife—or as good as.'

'I'm sure Anne knows that,' Yorke said easily.

'I just like to get things straight,' Jack Coram replied. 'You know what women are like when they get a bee in their bonnet about a man.'

'I don't think Yorke or Beth are interested in your opinion of women.' Anne's voice was as cold as ice though the look she gave her husband was hot with temper. 'Yorke is head over heels in love and thinks that marriage will be a bed of roses.'

'Perhaps it will be for him,' Jack Coram replied. 'Beth isn't as thorny as you!'

Yorke gave a soft laugh and looked at Beth. 'She certainly isn't. She doesn't even have any thorns. Nor hardly any leaves with which to protect herself.'

'Just a tender little bud,' Anne commented.

Beth clenched her hands at her sides and wished both Yorke and Anne could be consigned to some deep, impenetrable hole. With Jack Coram too, she thought, and wondered why, if he was so jealous of Anne, he had brought her here. More important still, why was he making it possible for Yorke to pursue his career at Powys?

A light touch on her elbow made her realise Yorke was leading her towards the other side of the room, on the pretext of getting her a drink. 'I'm sorry you had to be party to such a scene,' he apologised.

'The first of many, I should think. Our engagement won't work, Yorke. It isn't fooling anybody.'

'Keep a smile on your face,' he ordered, 'or people will think we're quarrelling.'

'It's impossible to quarrel with you. You never listen to me.'

'Then relax and let me make the decisions.' His glance rested on the creamy shoulders that rose from the scooped out neckline of her turquoise dress. 'Try and act as cool and confident as you look.'

'I could hit you!' she muttered mutinously.

'If you do, I'll kiss you in front of everybody. That way they'll know for sure it's a lovers' quarrel!'

She made an irritated gesture with her hand. 'You're buying time, Yorke, and I hate being a party to it. Anne will leave her husband the moment it suits her, and once she's free, you'll never be able to resist her.'

'I have more confidence in myself than *you* have in me,' he said dryly.

'So much confidence that you needed me to bolster it up for you.'

'A poor bolster too.' He leaned close and his breath

warmed the side of her neck. 'Why not marry me, Beth, and become my permanent prop? Or don't you find it appealing to become a marchioness?'

'I'd love the title,' she lied, 'but I don't like the man who comes with it.'

Before he could reply, she pushed past him and ran on to the verandah, then sped down the steps and round the back of the house, not caring where she went, only knowing she had to be alone.

CHAPTER TWELVE

ALONE in the deepening African dusk Beth returned to a semblance of her normal composure. It had been childish to give way to a display of temper with Yorke. After all, he was not responsible for the actions of Rowena or Anne. As she thought this she knew it was not true, for against his will Yorke was the catalyst in the lives of both the women; as he was the catalyst in hers. How empty her life would be when he was no longer a part of it, when she would have to face each day knowing she would never see him.

An insect buzzed round her hair and she shook her head and moved away from the shadow of a tree. Behind her she heard the chink of glasses and laughter and she walked further away from it, turning in the direction of the wooden fence that ran around the entire Centre. How like a Western film the setting was! All it needed was a few cowboys to come riding in through the gates. Yet outside lay no range with innocent cattle, but thousand of acres where wild beasts roamed free: enormous African elephants with their huge flapping ears and long swinging trunks; the graceful giraffe; the bad-tempered zebra who looked so beautiful galloping across the wide stretches of country and the tawny-haired lions like overgrown pussy cats. Unbidden she remembered the lion and lioness she had seen lying in the sun during her drive with John Stallard. How tenderly the lion had shown his affection towards his mate, so tenderly that it had aroused similar thoughts in John. No lion he, but a far more gentle animal. She sighed. Even without knowing Yorke she could never have married John. Intimacy without love was not for her and never could be.

'That's the third sigh in less than a minute.'

She spun round and saw Jack Coram. He was standing a yard away from her, rocking slowly backwards and forwards on the balls of his feet. Out in the open he looked smaller and chunkier than ever, but there was no denying the sheer bulldog tenacity to be seen in the heavy shoulders, the bullet-shaped head and the thick but firm jaw.

'I guess you came out here to get away from everyone,' he continued.

'Can you blame me?'

'Heck no. I'm sorry for what happened back there. I don't usually lose my temper with Anne—and never before in public.'

'You don't need to apologise to me, Mr Coram.'

'Make it Jack. We'll be seeing a lot of each other in the future.'

'I hope not,' she said, and then stopped, aghast at her tactlessness. But it was enough to break the tension and he chuckled deeply.

'I hope you don't go around saying what you think to everyone? They might not be as understanding as I am.'

'I didn't mean it in the way it sounded.'

His expression grew speculative. 'What did you mean, then?'

She bit her lip, knowing it was impossible to explain she would not be seeing him at Powys because she had no intention of remaining there once the arrangements for the Coram Institute had been completed.

'Don't tell me you and Yorke won't be living at Powys?' he questioned. 'From what the Marchioness has been telling me, she's hoping he'll turn it into a real stately home and open it to the public.'

'I doubt if he'll ever do that,' Beth said quickly. 'He will be too busy with the—with your Institute.'

'*The* Institute,' Jack Coram corrected. 'Once I make the endowment, it will be run by a board of trustees, headed by Yorke.' The eyes squinted at her. 'Do you think that's too trusting of me?'

She shook her head and though she knew he was waiting for her to say something, she resolutely kept silent. He teetered backwards and forwards again and then stopped and banged a clenched fist into the open palm of his other hand.

'I'm not a fool, Beth! Your engagement to Yorke is about as real as Anne's love for me. Mind you, I appreciate the effort Yorke is making to keep her out of his life, but he won't succeed.'

'What do you mean?'

'She always gets what she wants—and she wants Yorke.'

Beth moistened her lips and made the effort to speak. 'You talk as—as if I don't count with him.'

'Do you?' he asked heavily.

She ignored the question and asked one of her own. 'If you feel ... I mean, why are you giving Yorke the opportunity of going back to England?'

'Because I want to force Anne to make a decision. She believes she wants Yorke, but if he went on working here she'd never do anything about it. If I make it possible for him to work and live in England, she'll have the chance of coming to terms with herself.'

'I still don't understand,' Beth whispered.

'I'm tired of fighting someone's dream,' he said

bluntly, 'and I'm banking on the fact that Yorke doesn't love her.'

'If you think that, why didn't you let him prove it here at Mandama?'

'If he turned Anne down out here she'd say it was because he didn't think they would be happy together in Africa. But if he's back at Powys and he still doesn't want her, she will finally accept that he doesn't love her.'

'Or that he won't take another man's wife. There are some people who still look on marriage as a binding contract.'

'Anne isn't one of them,' Jack Coram said dryly, 'and when a man is in love, he isn't either.' He came a step closer. 'It must be hard for you to stand on the sidelines and wait to see what Yorke will do. I hope we both win.'

Beth shrugged. 'Yorke hoped his engagement to me would set your mind at rest.'

'Only Anne will be able to do that.'

'Won't you be bitter if Yorke does decide that he loves her?'

'You mean after I've given him the Institute?' Jack Coram shook his head. 'I want Anne to be happy. I'm a fool where she's concerned. The way Yorke is a fool with you.'

'With me?' she queried.

'For not knowing you love him. The engagement may be an act for him, but it means a lot to you.'

'He must never know,' she said quickly.

'I won't tell him. All I'm concerned with is the end of my own little play. I've set the stage, got the two main characters facing each other and I've written their lines in dollar bills! Now I'll wait for the finale.'

'Doesn't your wife realise that you know what she's planning to do?' Beth asked.

'Anne thinks I'm blind,' he said wryly. 'But for my money, I'm doing the best thing possible. If Yorke wants her, at least I'll know where I stand in the future. And if he turns her down, she'll come back to me a wiser woman.'

Beth had grave doubts about the latter part of his remark, but knew it would be heartless to say it. In a man who had so few illusions about the woman he loved, it would be a shame to destroy the only remaining one.

'When is the final act of the play?' she asked.

'My lawyers are meeting me in London at the end of the week with all the documents. Once I've signed them, the Coram Institute becomes a fact. Then I'll tell Anne she can have her freedom and the rest is up to her and Yorke.'

'He needn't have bothered getting engaged to me,' Beth said huskily. 'He only did it because——'

'He wanted to keep Anne off his neck until I was committed. But once I am, he'll be free to do as he wants.'

'Conscience permitting,' she said.

The man shrugged. 'Like I said before, a man in love has no conscience.'

Quietly he went away but, left to herself, Beth's thoughts were far from quiet and, in a turmoil of anxiety she paced the grass, a slim wraith-like figure among the foliage. Was Jack Coram right in his belief that Yorke would succumb to Anne once the institute became a fact? Or was the Texan judging Yorke on the way he himself would behave in a similar situation? And what of Yorke? Did he believe he had sufficient strength to ward off a woman as determined as Anne? At the moment he had put up the barricade of a false engagement, but what would he do when the engagement came to an end? This thought led to another that left her breathless. What if Yorke intended marriage? He had not mentioned it, but this did not mean it was not in his mind. Knowing how reluctant she had been to participate in his deception, he might have decided that to suggest marriage would frighten her so much that she would never have agreed to an engagement in the first place.

But now that she was engaged to him, he might believe he had sufficient power to persuade her to go along with him in an even greater deception. Yet marriage was a much more binding contract: in her eyes a totally binding one and not to be entered into except with sincerity. If only she knew what was in Yorke's mind. Yet despite his easy-going manner and charm—possibly because of it—she could not even begin to understand how he felt. If he regretted the decision he had made five years ago, he now had a chance to rectify it—providing his conscience would allow him to take another man's wife. Beth shook her head. Once more her thoughts had gone in a full circle and she was still no nearer finding a solution. A trickle of sweat ran down her temple and she wiped it away, realising at the same time that her whole skin was damp. How hot and sultry it was, even at an hour when it was supposed to be cool. She longed for the comfort of an air-conditioned room and thought longingly of her own bedroom. But it was impossible to leave the party and slowly she retraced her steps. The nearer she came to John Stallard's house, the louder grew the noise and the more reluctant she became to become part of it.

'I was coming to look for you.' Yorke's voice made her start with surprise and she saw him walking across the grass towards her. How cool and imperturbable he looked in a suit that showed no crease and a crisp white shirt that showed none of the limpness of heat.

'I came out for a breath of air.'

His glance took in her perspiring face. 'You look as if you're about to drop from heat stroke.'

'I went for a walk,' she said. 'It was foolish of me.'

'You do many foolish things. Running off from the party was one of them.'

'I wanted to be alone.'

'Your thoughts followed you, though,' he said quietly, 'and it doesn't look as if they were pleasant ones.'

'Stop treating me as if I'm one of your experimental monkeys!'

'You are a very pretty one,' he said mildly, and leaned against the wooden balustrade to look at her. It was a look that made her heart turn over and she was painfully aware of his nearness.

'Would you like to lie down for a bit?' His question startled her and though she instinctively shook her head, she then changed her mind and nodded. Seeing it, he put his hand on her arm and led her away from the house. After a few paces she realised he was not taking her back to her rondavel but to his own, and she stopped walking.

'I don't want to go to your room, Yorke.'

'You won't be disturbed there. My grandmother has already left the party,' he added by way of explanation, 'and if you leave early too, she'll want to know why.'

'I could tell her the truth,' Beth replied. 'It's cruel to let her go on building up false hopes about us.'

'They needn't be false.'

She caught her breath. At last it came. 'What does that mean?' she asked with innocence.

'We could get married,' he said.

'No, we can't.'

'Why not? You liked me when we first met. I'll take a chance on your getting to like me again.'

'Never,' she said passionately. 'I wouldn't marry you if you were the last man on earth.'

'Don't talk in clichés,' he said crisply.

'Then stop acting like one! Don't run into the arms of one woman to stop you running into the arms of another. You should have proposed to Rowena,' she went on furiously. 'She would have been more delighted to turn the pretence into reality.'

'You know why I didn't want Rowena.'

'Because she would have intruded on your thoughts of Anne,' Beth cried, 'and because you couldn't pacify her the way you think you can pacify me.'

'I don't seem to be pacifying you very well,' he said wryly. 'I suppose you blame me because you've lost Stallard?'

For a second she looked at him blankly, then she clutched at his words like a drowning man at a straw. 'Why shouldn't I blame you? He was a kind and intelligent man who would have made a wonderful husband.'

'For you, for Rowena or for any other woman who indicated her availability.'

'That's not fair,' she stormed. 'He's been a widower for years.'

'But he only recently decided on remarriage,' Yorke said quietly, 'and you came on the scene at the right time. But if it can't be you, then any other young presentable woman will do.'

Beth clamped her lips shut. Yorke's words hurt, but they were obviously true.

'Come on,' Yorke said roughly. 'You look as if you're going to faint!' Half dragging her, he led her across the compound to his rondavel. The interior was cool and dim and she sank down gratefully in an armchair and closed her eyes. A moment later she felt a glass placed in her hand.

'Drink up,' he ordered.

She obeyed, pulling a face at the bitter tasting liquid though she did not ask him what it was. Several moments passed and the swift beating of her heart steadied. She opened her eyes and sat up. For an instant she thought she was alone, then she saw Yorke leaning against the side of the window, his profile towards her. He was unaware of her watching him and she saw how serious he looked and how sad.

'I feel better now, thank you,' she said composedly, and stood up.

'Don't go,' he said abruptly. 'There's no need to return to the party. They won't miss us—and even if they do, they won't find it odd that we prefer to be alone.'

'I would rather not stay here.'

'Why not?' He strode over to her, his face livid. 'Every time I look at you, you act as if I'm going to rape you! I put my hand on your arm and you shake like a leaf. If I——'

'I don't like you,' she interrupted. 'That's why.'

'That isn't why,' he denied. 'Your lips say one thing but your eyes say another. And so does your body,' he said, putting his hands on her waist. 'You're trembling, Beth, but it isn't with fright. It's with desire.'

Pulling her close, he wrapped his arms round her, pressing his body against the length of hers so that she felt every part of him: his heart thudding against her breasts, the flat tenseness of his stomach, the weight of his thighs and the wild upsurge of passion that he could not control and made no effort to hide.

It was impossible for her to resist his need, for it awakened such an answering response that her fear evaporated and she clung to him with an abandon she had not shown until now, twining her arms round his neck and pulling his head lower to enjoy the bruising power of his mouth. She wanted him and she did not care if he knew it. She was tired of pretending. It was pointless to think about tomorrow when tomorrow was only going to be dreary and lonely. She would concentrate today—tonight—and take what Yorke was offering. At least it would give her memories to look back on.

'Yorke,' she muttered, and clung to him.

His hands fumbled at the back of her dress and there was the rasp of the zip as the soft folds of linen fell at her feet. His fingers caressed the smooth skin of her back as she clung even closer as he picked her up and carried her over to the divan, not lifting his mouth from hers as he placed her on it and lay beside her. Then his head lay upon her breast and his mouth was warm on the swelling curves which swelled even more at his touch. She moaned and convulsively grasped at him, her hands stroking the strong muscles that rippled along his shoulders. He gave a shudder and gripped her so tightly that she thought her ribs would crack and then, astonishingly, he pushed himself away and stood up.

In the dimness she could not see his face, but his voice was low and without inflection. 'I'm sorry, Beth. You were right to be afraid of me. I'll take you back to your room.'

Silently she stood up. Her dress lay in a heap on the floor and she stepped into it, aware of how naked she must look in brief panties and the wisp of lace which lifted her breasts without covering them. But she was beyond being embarrassed by his look, so overwhelmed was she by the knowledge that she had wanted to give him everything, and would have done so if he had not been the one to resist. Her fingers shook so much that she could not do up the zip, and silently he came behind her and did it for her.

His nearness was more than she could bear, and with a strangled cry she ran from the room, uncaring that he called her name, knowing only that she never wanted to see him again.

CHAPTER THIRTEEN

FOR the next few days Beth avoided being alone with Yorke. It was made easier by the fact that he was with John Stallard, Jack Coram and the other two Texans.

'I can't believe Yorke is finally leaving Mandama,' the Marchioness said the night before they were due to leave for England. 'It has all happened with such speed.'

'You must thank Mr Coram for that,' said Beth.

'I do. And I thank you too.' The sharp eyes softened as they rested on Beth's slight form. 'You must be pleased at the way things have turned out. You love Powys almost as much as I do.'

Beth nodded and bent over the case she was packing.

'When are you and Yorke planning to get married?' the Marchioness asked. 'I hope you won't keep me waiting too long. I want to see a great-grandchild before I die.'

Beth lifted her head, wondering if she dared tell the Marchioness the truth. Yet she could not bring herself to destroy the woman's illusions. When her engagement ended she would leave Powys and let Yorke explain the facts to his grandmother. Like a Bedouin she would steal away into the night and, like a Bedouin, she would roam for the rest of her life.

Later that day a small aircraft took them to Johannesburg, a repetition of the flight they had made a few short weeks ago. John Stallard bade her a personal goodbye, managing to escape from Rowena's proprietorial hold in order to do so. But he said nothing that could not have been overheard by anyone else, though there was a look in his eyes that told her he regretted her refusal of him.

'I hope we will meet again in the future,' he said, and she smiled and nodded, knowing full well that they would never meet again and glad of it.

Only when they boarded the plane and lifted off into the sky did she feel the first stirring of freedom, though she knew she would not be finally free until she had said goodbye to Yorke. He was sitting across the aisle from her, pointing out a herd of impala to Jack Coram who was photographing them with a movie camera. Anne was sitting next to the Marchioness who, since Yorke's engagement, had unbent sufficiently to pretend to a surface relationship with her. As if aware of Beth's eyes, Anne turned and gave her a derisive look, but it was not until later that night that she put the look into words.

Beth had gone down to the lobby of the hotel in search of something to read; she had retired early with the Marchioness, using it as an excuse to avoid conversation with Yorke and the Corams, and regretted the bad luck that made Anne spot her by the bookstall.

'If you aren't tired, why don't you join us?' Anne said.

'I prefer to stay with the Marchioness.'

'You can't act the companion once you're Yorke's wife. Or have you faced up to the fact that you never will be?' Beth went to move away, but Anne refused to step aside. 'He's mine,' she insisted, 'and he will never belong to you or anyone else.'

'What are you going to do? Make him wear a ball and chain?'

'Marry him.' Anne smiled mockingly. 'Jack won't prevent me and it's only your phoney engagement that has to be finished.'

'If marriage lines don't bother you, I'm surprised at

your letting an engagement stand in your way.' Beth pushed Anne unceremoniously out of the way and retreated across the lobby. So Jack had conceded the battle lost. She refused to think of what the final outcome might be, though she could not help a measure of sadness at the way the Marchioness would react. But perhaps in the long run it would not matter. Yorke would be working at Powys no matter what happened, and marriage either to her or Anne would, as far as the old lady was concerned, amount to the same thing.

Like a jewel in a sea of green, Powys stood in its lush acres welcoming them home.

'A good night's sleep for all of us,' Jack Coram said to Yorke, 'and tomorrow we can get down to the contracts.'

'If I know American ones, we'll have a week of reading ahead of us,' Yorke smiled.

'This isn't a businesss deal,' said Coram. 'There will be no fancy clauses and hidden meanings. All my lawyers are concerned with is making sure I can endow the money without giving myself any tax headaches, and to make sure that my estate will support the Foundation if anything happens to me.'

Yorke gave a slight shake of his head. 'I still can't believe it's barely a fortnight since you came to Africa. So much has happened in a short time.'

'I should have come to Africa years ago,' Coram replied. 'A lot of things might have been different then.' His small eyes rested on Anne but she seemed uncaring and, with a shrug, he went towards the stairs. 'Coming, Anne?'

She followed, glancing at Yorke as she did so. She made a lovely picture as she stood momentarily at the foot of the stairs, the dark panelling framing her silver fairness and the solid furniture a perfect foil for her graceful figure. How at home she looked in this setting, Beth thought, and would have given a great deal to know if Yorke thought so too. But he gave no sign of it and remained the polite host as he escorted the Corams to their room.

'I'll be down again in a moment,' he said to Beth over his shoulder.

'I'm tired too,' she replied, 'so I'll say goodnight now.'

'All right, darling.'

His tone was so lover-like that it dismayed her. If Yorke was capable of such subterfuge, how could any woman ever know where she was with him? Still, that wasn't to be her problem, and it was one which Anne was worldly enough not to care about.

In her own room, which had a delightful view across the fields to the cliffs, Beth wished she could photograph it indelibly on her mind, for no picture could ever hope to mirror the scene completely. Her glance strayed to the copse. In a matter of weeks a thick swathe of trees would be felled to make way for the Institute. How happy Yorke would be, to watch his dreams take shape and reality. Dr Yorke Powys—that was what he really was. His inheritance came a far second in his life, so she could not blame him for it. Was it the title Anne wanted or the man? Maybe it was a combination of both. The memory of Yorke's touch still burned on her and she turned hurriedly from the window. As soon as the contracts had been signed, she must leave.

For the whole of the next day Yorke and Jack Coram were closeted in the library with the two lawyers who had flown in from Houston and Yorke's own legal adviser who had travelled down from London. Anne was in a state of tension and unable to stay in one place for more than a few moments.

If the Marchioness was aware of the girl's agitation she gave no sign of it and proceeded on her daily routine as though nothing momentous was taking place in the library. And it *was* momentous, Beth knew, for the Institute would bring a new way of life to Powys, turning it from a mere stately home—an anachronism in the twentieth century world—into a living force with a future of importance.

At four o'clock the discussions were still going on, and the old lady glanced at the closed door as though tempted to go in and see what was happening. Instead she occupied herself by playing cards with Beth, who deliberately allowed her to win, a fact which did not escape the bright black eyes.

'Put up a fight, girl,' she exclaimed. 'I hate an easy victory.'

'Beth is no fighter,' said Anne, coming up to the card table. 'She's wise enough to know when to give in.'

'One should never give in,' the Marchioness snapped. 'It is a sign of weakness.'

Beth said nothing since the two women were talking at cross purposes, although she knew Anne's words were directed at her, each one carefully aimed to hurt.

At six o'clock the men came out of the library and, seeing their faces flushed and smiling, the Marchioness signalled Beth to ask the butler to bring in the magnum of champagne which had been resting on ice for several hours.

'All signed!' Jack Coram exclaimed. 'Even if I die tomorrow my name will live on. I must say I never thought it would be because of a laboratory. I always saw myself as a patron of the arts.'

'Art patrons are two a penny,' the Marchioness snorted. The champagne was poured and glasses were raised. Beth tried to keep out of the conversation, but one of the American lawyers buttonholed her to talk about Powys and the magnificent books he had barely had time to glance at in the library.

'With a house like this I can understand why the Marquis wanted to come back,' he said. 'Tradition is something we don't have in the States, leastways not of this kind. I wish I'd had more time to look at everything.' The lawyer sipped his champagne. 'I never thought we would conclude the negotiations so quickly.'

'Does Mr Coram always work so fast?'

'He generally likes to have things done yesterday. The word "tomorrow" isn't part of his vocabulary!'

'Endowing the Coram Institute is investing in a lot of tomorrows,' Beth said, and glanced over to the man they were discussing. He was talking to Yorke but looking at Anne, who was a picture of loveliness in her favourite red. Even as Beth watched, the Texan looked at his wrist watch and beckoned his lawyer over.

'We'd better be going,' he said loudly, 'otherwise we'll miss our train.'

'Going?' the Marchioness asked blankly. 'But I assumed you would all be dining here.'

Jack Coram glanced at Yorke, who looked apologetically at his grandmother.

'I'm afraid it slipped my mind to tell you, but Jack sprang it on me that he has to get back to London.'

'I'll be staying on, though,' said Anne.

The Marchioness looked at Beth, who murmured that she would go and inform the butler of the change of plans. Outside the door she leaned for a moment against the wall to regain her strength. Jack Coram was obviously not wasting any time in putting his wife to the test. He was leaving the field clear for Yorke to make his decision. And now she had to do the same. Yet in her case it would not be leaving Yorke to make a decision, it would just be leaving him. For no matter what he decided to do, she could never be part of his life. If he wanted a future with Anne then her own presence here would be an embarrassment, and if he turned Anne down, she was not going to let him use her as a barricade again. Panic urged her to leave Powys immediately, and only the fact that it would mean travelling on the same train as Jack Coram—and having to face his sympathy —decided her to leave in the morning instead. This settled, she felt a deep sense of relief, and when she returned to the drawing-room she was content in the knowledge that she would only have to pretend for a further few hours.

Jack was already making his farewells. He seemed to have arranged everything extremely well, for his cases were packed and waiting for him in the hall and his goodbye to his wife was laconic, as though he anticipated seeing her in a couple of days.

'When are you returning to the States?' the Marchioness asked as he gallantly kissed her hand.

'At the end of the week.'

'So soon?'

'I've done what I came over to do.'

'A great deal more,' one of his lawyers interposed. 'Four million dollars, to be precise.'

'You will be back, of course?' the Marchioness added.

'I hope so.' The Texan moved over to Beth. His eyes tried to tell her something, but she refused to read the message. 'If you ever come to Texas,' he said softly, 'look me up.' Then he turned to his wife. 'I'll be at the

Savoy, honey. That part of my plan hasn't changed.'

Unexpectedly Anne leaned forward and kissed his cheek. He gripped her on the shoulder and then pushed her away, striding out without a backward glance. Yorke went into the hall to see him off and the three women were left alone. The Marchioness looked from Beth to Anne as though aware something was wrong but not sure what it was.

'Why aren't you returning to London with your husband?' she asked, her voice more hesitant than usual.

'I left Powys too quickly last time,' Anne answered, 'and I don't intend to make the same mistake again.'

'That was five years ago. Things have changed since then.'

'Only for the better.'

'If we're going to change for dinner,' Beth put in hastily, and stepped between the Marchioness and Anne, afraid that unless she did so, too much would be given away. Tomorrow her employer would have to know the truth, but by then she would be miles away.

'Come upstairs with me, child.' The Marchioness rested with unusual heaviness on Beth's arm, drawing a look of enquiry from her.

'It might be better for you to have dinner in bed,' she suggested.

'I think you're right. Today has been more exciting than I realised. Yes, I will take a rest.' She glanced at Anne. 'I am sure you will be able to manage without me.'

'Of course.' Anne eyed Beth. 'Will you be having dinner with the Marchioness?'

'Of course she won't,' the old lady snapped. 'Yorke will be so pleased with himself tonight he'll want Beth to celebrate with him.'

Only when she was upstairs did the Marchioness give any sign that she had understood the meaning behind Anne's suggestion. 'She still hasn't given up hope of getting Yorke back. The sooner you marry him the better.'

Beth silently unclasped the triple row of pearls from around the crepey neck and placed it on the dressing table. 'If Yorke wasn't engaged to you I would feel quite differently, of course, and then I would be frightened. Set the date, child, and put my mind at rest. I don't want that harpy to get him.'

'You talk as if Mrs Coram is a stranger,' Beth said. 'After all, you welcomed her into your family five years ago.'

'I hadn't met you then. You will make him a far better wife, and his feelings for you are quite different, you know. It isn't the same sort of passion he had for Anne. He looks at you with such tenderness.'

Beth moved quickly to the door. 'I'll see about your dinner,' she said, and hurried out before she gave way to her misery.

How blind the Marchioness was if she imagined Yorke looked at her with tenderness. But then perhaps wanting to believe something made one see things that weren't there. Yet even though she herself wanted Yorke desperately, she had never seen love or tenderness in his eyes.

Beth toyed with the idea of not going down to dinner that night. After all, she was leaving tomorrow, so what was the point of carrying on the pretence for a few more hours? Yet a determination not to let Anne know she had won so easily finally made her put on one of her prettiest dresses and go slowly down the wide staircase to the drawing-room. Because of her indecision she was later than usual and she knew Anne was already with

Yorke as she crossed the hall. The door was ajar, but her steps were muted on the carpet and neither of them were aware of her on the threshold.

'There's no need for you to go on pretending,' said Anne. 'Jack knows I love you and he told me he won't stand in our way.'

'You've taken a lot of things for granted.' Yorke's voice was more jerky than Beth had ever heard it, as though he were labouring under great emotional stress.

'I love you,' Anne said, 'and all I've done is to go on believing that you love me. I should never have left you years ago. I behaved like a child.'

'You're still behaving like a child. I'm engaged to Beth.'

'For heaven's sake, don't go on with that charade! Now all the papers have been signed Jack can't back out even if he wanted to.'

'Do you think I was waiting for everything to be signed before coming to claim you? Is that what Coram thinks too?'

'Naturally. And so did Jack. He knows I've never stopped regretting what I did. He wants me to be happy,' she cried. 'That's why he's founded the Institute.'

'He's willing to spend a considerable amount of money to buy your happiness,' Yorke said thinly. 'I hadn't realised he saw things so clearly.'

'He's no fool.' Anne came to stand beside him. 'Face the facts, darling, and stop worrying about hurting Jack. He had me for five years too many and now I can be yours.' She curved into his arms. 'I've waited so long for you, Yorke. We deserve to be happy.'

'Anne.' Yorke's voice was thick with emotion and Beth backed away and ran for the stairs. She did not stop running until she was in the safety of her room and even then she could not rest. Feverishly she pulled her clothes out of the wardrobe and drawers and flung them into her suitcase, uncaring of the jumble they made. Her books were thrown on top and her shoes on top of them. Thank goodness she did not have much to pack. She slammed the lock shut and only as she heard it click into place did she wonder where she was going to go. She had already missed the London train, but she was sure there was another one which would get her to the city in the early hours of the morning. It would mean a long uncomfortable journey, but anything was better than remaining here.

Picking up her suitcase, she tiptoed down the corridor to the back stairs. She dared not run the risk of going down to the main hall in case Yorke and Anne saw her. Only as she reached the servants' lobby did she realise she had not written goodbye to the Marchioness. But she was afraid to go back to her room and do it in case Yorke came in search of her to see why she had not put in an appearance for dinner. She would have to write from London. It would be morning before her absence was discovered and by then Yorke would be able to tell his grandmother the truth.

Beth reached the small local station with an hour to spare before the night train to London arrived. The porter looked at her curiously since he knew who she was, although news of her engagement to the Marquis had not yet been officially announced.

'I've locked the waiting room for the night,' he said. 'We weren't expecting any passengers. But you'll find it more comfortable to sit in my room. There's a heater there and a radio if you want it.'

Unwilling to tell him she would prefer to be alone, she followed him into his office and took the easy chair he indicated, while he busied himself filling in forms at his desk and making a couple of telephone calls relating to a goods train that was standing at a junction further up the line.

'Looks like I'll have to go and see the train myself,' he said to Beth. 'A valuable parcel was put aboard it by mistake and I have to collect it. But I've switched the station phone through to my assistant's house, so you won't be disturbed by any calls.'

He hurried out and with a feeling of relief, Beth relaxed. The room seemed strangely quiet and she looked around it, forcing herself to concentrate on what she saw for fear she might concentrate on what she remembered. But it was impossible to shut out memories and she buried her head in her hands and muttered Yorke's name over and over again.

'Are you reciting a dirge or a litany?' a grave voice asked, and with a startled cry she jerked up her head and saw Yorke in front of her.

'What are you doing here?' she whispered.

'I don't need to ask *you* that question.'

She said nothing and turned her head away, hoping he would leave her yet knowing he wouldn't. 'What do you want of me, Yorke?'

'The truth—without fabrication. I take it it was you I heard coming down the stairs earlier this evening?' he continued, and waited for her nod. 'I thought so,' he said on a sigh, 'but by the time I got into the hall, you must have dashed back to your room.'

'I didn't know you'd heard me. I thought you were too occupied.'

'How much of my conversation with Anne did you hear?' he demanded.

'Enough to know it was time for me to leave.'

'Not quite enough, I'm afraid. If you'd heard it all, you would have known it was not the time for you to go.'

She heard him move and only as she felt his breath on her cheek did she realise he had bent down towards her.

'Look at me, Beth. I want to see your eyes when I speak to you.'

She refused to obey his command and his hand came out and gripped her chin, forcing her to face him. She lowered her lids, but then as she heard his soft intake of breath, she raised them again.

'That's better,' he said huskily, staring into them. 'I've let you run away from me too many times. Tonight there will be no more running; or at least if you do so, it will be for the last time, because I will never come after you again.'

'I didn't ask you to come after me now,' she said angrily, 'and I wish you would go away.'

'Because you hate me or because you love me?'

This time she did close her eyes, for it was the only way she could stop him from seeing her tears.

'Do you love me or hate me?' he repeated.

'Does it matter?' she cried.

'More than anything in the world. For heaven's sake, Beth, don't you know what I'm trying to tell you?'

Unbelievingly she stared at him. His skin was flushed and his eyes glittered in a way she had never seen before. 'But Anne?' she whispered. 'You love her.'

'Not that again,' he groaned, and pulled her to her feet and into his arms. 'I stopped loving her a long time ago, but I didn't realise it finally until I saw her again.' He frowned. 'No, that isn't true either. Once I met you, I was pretty sure I had stopped caring about her. But you were so difficult to convince that I finally began to doubt my own feelings.'

'Once you met *me*?' she echoed, repeating the only words that made sense to her.

'You,' he said huskily. 'From the moment I saw you at the airport I loved you. You were so small and slender, yet you had fire in your eyes.'

'I reminded you of Anne,' Beth said, and tried to push him away. 'That's the only reason I appealed to you.'

'You're nothing like Anne,' he said, refusing to let her go.

'That isn't true. You told me yourself I made you think of her.'

'I didn't mean it the way you thought. I meant that seeing you had made me realise my love for her had been a mirage. You are everything I had believed Anne to be and then discovered that she wasn't. It isn't just the outward physical you that I love but what you are inside. Your character and personality. The way you think and act—though you've been acting and thinking like a crazy woman for weeks on end!' He tilted her chin and looked deep into her eyes. 'I tried to tell you this so many times, but you didn't seem able to understand.'

'I was too busy hearing what everybody else was saying,' she said shakily. 'Rowena, Anne—even John.'

At the mention of John, Yorke's eyes narrowed. 'What did he mean to you, Beth?'

'Nothing except a subterfuge,' she confessed, and was rewarded by the smile that curved his lips.

'I thought so, but I wanted to hear you say it.' He touched her cheek with his finger. 'I'm not wrong in thinking you care for me, am I?'

'I don't care for you,' she whispered. 'I adore you.'

'Love at first sight,' he said whimsically, 'yet what a lot of time we've wasted realising it.'

'I still haven't realised it,' she admitted. 'I'm afraid I'll wake up and find it's all a dream.'

'You nearly turned it into a nightmare,' he said, giving her a shake. 'How dared you leave me to cope with Anne alone tonight?'

'What happened?' Beth asked.

'I finally got her to see I loved *you* and that my engagement—far from being a cover to pull over Coram's eyes—was a cover to pull over yours.'

'Mine?' Beth said indignantly.

'Of course. Pleading for your help was the only way I could think up to get you to become engaged to me. I was pretty sure you weren't indifferent to me, yet for some reason best known to yourself, you were letting John make sheep's eyes at you. Making you my temporary fiancée seemed a marvellous idea at the time.'

'Not any more?' she asked demurely.

'Now I can think of something better for you to be,' he said against her mouth. 'My very permanent and loved wife.'

With a murmur of ecstasy Beth gave herself up to his kiss, responding to it without subterfuge and revelling in the intensity of his desire. Again and again he drained her mouth of its sweetness and they were both visibly shaken by the time she pulled slightly back from him.

'Where is Anne now?' she asked, knowing it was something she had to be told.

'The last I saw of her she was racing upstairs to pack and my chauffeur was driving her to London. She should be with her husband by the morning.'

'He will take her back too,' Beth said soberly.

'They might stand a chance of being happy together now that she's realised she can't turn back the clock again.' Yorke touched his lips to her hair. 'No more

188

doubts, my darling. You are the only woman I want as my wife.'

'I still can't think why. I'm so ordinary and you're so ... Oh, Yorke, why me?'

'I'll tell you why, my angel,' he said, gathering her close, 'but even beginning now, it's going to take me the next fifty years!'

'Start,' she said huskily, her mouth on his. 'Start, Yorke, and never stop.'

Now available!

COLLECTION EDITIONS

of Harlequin Romances

Harlequin is proud to present this collection of the best-selling romance novels of former years. It's a rare series of 100 books, each one reissued in a beautifully designed new cover. And the cost is only 75¢ each.

Not sold in stores

Send for free catalog

Most of these old favorites have not been reissued since first publication. So if you read them then, you'll enjoy them again; if they're new to you, you'll have the pleasure of discovering a new series of compelling romances from past years.

Collection Editions are available only from Harlequin Reader Service. They are not sold in stores.

Clip and mail this special coupon. We will send you a catalog listing all the Collection Editions titles and authors.

Harlequin Reader Service
MPO Box 707,
Niagara Falls, N.Y. 14302

In Canada:
Stratford, Ontario
N5A 6W4

Please send me, without obligation, your free Collection Editions catalog containing 100 vintage Harlequin romance novels.

NAME _____
(please print)

ADDRESS _____

CITY _____

STATE/PROV. _____ ZIP/POSTAL CODE _____

Offer expires December 31, 1977

PRS 188.

Send for your copy today

The Harlequin Romance Catalog FREE!

Here's your chance to catch up on all the wonderful Harlequin Romance novels you may have missed because the books are no longer available at your favorite booksellers.

Complete the coupon and mail it to us. By return mail, we'll send you a copy of the latest Harlequin catalog. Then you'll be able to order the books you want directly from us.

Clip and mail coupon today.

Harlequin Reader Service
M.P.O. Box 707
Niagara Falls, N.Y. 14302

In Canada:
Harlequin Reader Service
Stratford, Ontario   N5A 6W4

Please send my FREE
Harlequin Romance Catalog!

NAME _____

ADDRESS _____

CITY _____

STATE }
PROV. }   ZIP }
        POSTAL CODE }   PRS 188